ALWAYS ON HIS MIND

THE BRIDES OF PURPLE HEART RANCH BOOK 7

SHANAE JOHNSON

THOSE JOHNSON GIRLS

CONTENTS

Edited by Alyssa Breck

Manufactured in the United States of America
First Edition June 2019

CHAPTER ONE

He was dreaming, of that he was sure.

But it was one of those dreams where he felt every sensation. The heat of the fire licked up his back as though his spine was a trail of gasoline. Sharp pebbles and debris bit at the fleshy underside of his palms and nipped at the cleft of his chin. The ear-piercing screams of women beat at his eardrum like the percussive section of a marching band in a small auditorium.

Then came the blood. Metallic and musty. Tinged with a burning, chemical smell. The stench gripped his gut, forcing his stomach to surrender its goods.

He felt, heard, tasted, and smelled all of it. But he

saw nothing. All around him was a thick, suffocating blackness.

He was trapped in the darkness of his mind. Though he knew he was dreaming, he could not wake up. He could not move a limb, not even his pinky finger. Everything was bound, strapped down, and held tight. There was no escape.

His senses released their hold when voices rose around him in the darkness. He knew the urgent murmurs were not a part of the dream. The voices came from the real world.

The words were spoken in a foreign tongue. Harsh consonants, few vowel sounds. But he understood the meanings.

"We have to move him."

"It's too dangerous."

The voices were feminine, but there was steel in their tone. Whoever these women were, he knew they were very brave, strong, and capable. That knowledge would've made another man relax. Not him. He felt honor bound to rise to their aide.

The urge to reach out to them was a powerful one. He felt it was his responsibility to help them complete their mission. He got the sense that that was what he did. He completed missions, got things done.

Unfortunately, he couldn't do anything at the moment. He wasn't sure if his eyes were open? He was still bound in darkness. On the bright side, life was slowly returning to his limbs and extremities.

His right pinky separated from the rest of his fingers and wiggled. His head turned a fraction to the left. He took in a deep breath, feeling his chest rise high as his lungs expanded to their full capacity. And then it appeared.

A tiny light. Smaller than a pinprick. It grew to the size of a pencil tip. Then to the size of the surface of a spoon. Until, finally, it filled his eyes.

His eyes were definitely open now. He was awake, let loose from the dream world and his shadowy captivity. But there wasn't much to see.

The room he was in was dark. Just not the all-encompassing dark of the dream world. There were gradations of black from ebony to charcoal to slate gray.

His eyes were adjusting quickly now, and he began to pick apart his surroundings. There were more than two bodies standing over him. He couldn't make them out. Their heads and faces were covered in black cloth. Only their eyes were visible. But he knew they all were women.

"You are awake," one of them said. The language

she spoke switched. It was more familiar, easier on the ears to hear. Easier on his brain to understand.

"We will have to move him now. It is not safe if he stays."

"It is not safe if we move him."

"We will not have a choice much longer. They will come for him. We cannot continue to shelter him."

"But he saved our lives. We owe him."

The silence was tense. He could see the worry in the posture of one woman, the one insistent on sending him away from ... wherever he was. He saw defiance in the one who spoke up.

He opened his mouth, but only a garbled sound came out. His throat was on fire. Like a blaze burning in the dry desert.

"We need to send him back to his own people."

"We have already sent word. No one has come. We cannot wait any longer."

His people? He had people? He tried to picture who he belonged to, but his mind came up blank. Just a black slate. Not absolute darkness like the dream. Not as many gradations as this darkened room.

He tried to sit up, but a pain in his shoulder prevented it. Now that he thought of it, there was pain everywhere. He let out a strangled cry. The sound was short-lived as it burned a path through his throat and over his tongue.

All three women went tense. Their gazes went to the far side of the room where a tiny sliver of light escaped. That was the way out. Or the way in.

He shrank from that light. But a shard found him, landing on his bottom lip. His lips trembled under the weight of the ray.

Inside his mind, he felt the dream world pushing at the real world. He knew he could not let that happen. He could not let the sharp heat or the blood-curdling screams enter this world.

But the ray of light was unrelenting. It moved up his face, touching his upper lip, then his nose. He knew that if it got to his eyes, he would be in trouble. The eyes were the windows into the soul after all.

The women moved in front of him, blocking out the light. He breathed a sigh of relief at the narrow escape. But the reprieve was short-lived. Movement sounded from the crack where the light intruded.

The other two women stepped in front of him as well. The sight of the protective barrier in front of him kicked him into action. It should be him standing in front of them. But he couldn't rise. The pain in his limbs prevented it.

Even though he was still lying down, he wanted to shout at the women to get behind him. He wanted to rise from the bed to protect them. This was all wrong. He might not know much, but he knew that was his duty; to protect.

Before he could get any words out, the sliver of light grew. It invaded the room, spreading across the floor and taking up stations in the corners. And then they were inside.

Large men carrying guns burst into the room. He wasn't sure how many. They filled the entire space.

The women gasped. But just as soon as they gasped, relief seemed to rush through the room. One woman put her hand to her chest and began chanting in that harsh language. Another sank to her knees and bowed, beginning a prayer of gratitude. The third, the one who had fiercely tried to protect him, stepped forward.

One of the gun-toting men peered around her. He had dark hair and dark eyes. He was covered in tan clothing that looked familiar. The way the man looked him over, with relief, and gratitude and guilt, tugged at a memory in the darkness of his mind.

"Thank God, we found you, Private Cartwright."

CHAPTER TWO

"But I thought the highest worship of the Lord was love. Wouldn't that mean that if we got married, it would only prove our devotion to God?"

It was a good argument, thought Beth Barrett as she gazed at the young woman with a high ponytail and flowery, plastic barrettes in her hair. Too bad the voice making it was high-pitched with a nasally whine.

Beth sat in the Youth Pastor's office. She didn't sit behind the desk. She sat just off to the side, next to the youth pastor as he attempted to counsel the young couple before them. Beth wore a placid smile on her face as the two teens put forth their argument that they be allowed to marry without their parents' consent.

"We love each other, and we want to be together," the young girl said.

Her whine raised an octave on the last word. Beth winced at the dog whistle note. Luckily, she was able to cover her discomfort with a sigh she hoped would be translated as sympathetic.

Pastor Walter Vance smiled over at her. Though Beth wasn't sure if it was at her sigh? Or if he was appreciative of her faked compassion?

She assumed the latter when Walter steepled his fingers and nodded at the young man and woman. Nathaniel Green, the hopeful fiancé, sat upright, holding Nathalie Brown's hand.

Yes, that was their names. Nat Brown and Nat Green. The similarities in their names had pushed them together all their lives. With their last names being close in the alphabet they were often seated next to or near each other in the public schools of their small town. Nat and Nat started dating just before high school and had never stopped. A romantic person might call it fate. Their parents called it too soon.

"You know my hands are tied until you're both eighteen," said Walter.

"He *is* eighteen," Nathalie insisted.

"Yes, but you're not," Walter said patiently.

"I'm seventeen and three months old."

"Plenty of time to start planning a wedding," Beth added helpfully.

In response, Nathalie cut her with a death glare. Beth sat back in her seat and resumed her silence. She dropped the forced smile. She rarely had to force her smiles in church. Only when, as part of her duties as the pastor's daughter, she had to sit and listen to those who cared more about their way than what was right.

Luckily, Walter was there to pick up the gauntlet. "Even when you reach the age of majority, don't you want your parents' blessing?"

"They're never going to give it to us," said Nathaniel. "My mom wants me to go to college, get a degree, explore the world and other people."

"I love it here," Nathalie was saying. "I've never wanted to live anywhere but here. I've never wanted to be anything but a wife and a mom. Is that so bad?"

Natalie looked to Beth for an answer. Beth wished she disagreed with the young girl. But they had the exact same aspirations.

Beth had her Associate's degree, which she'd earned from courses at the local college. Unlike many of her former schoolmates, she had no desire to explore the world outside of their town. More than anything in the world, she wanted to be a wife and a mom.

Walter gazed down at her, as though he knew the trajectory of her thoughts. He covered her left hand with his, resting his thumb on the rock he'd put there not long ago.

"I'm a traditional woman like you, Nathalie," Beth said.

"Thank you," Nathalie exclaimed as though Beth had entirely cosigned her argument.

"But," Beth continued. "I couldn't imagine walking down the aisle without my father at my side. Can you?"

Nathalie pursed her lips and wrinkled her nose like the child she still was. "But don't you believe in love? Don't you know when it's true and the only thing you want?"

Beth did know all about that. She'd been in love since before she understood what the word meant. She'd felt the feelings the first time she'd laid eyes on the man of her dreams. She'd loved nothing more than gazing into his blue eyes.

Walter's smiling brown gaze settled on her,

shining with admiration. Beth cleared her throat, but words failed her.

"I mean, didn't you know that when you said yes to marrying Pastor Vance?"

Now all eyes were on her. Vocal Natalie, silent Nathaniel, patient Walter.

Beth was not a liar. What she was was a coward. She'd never told Reece Cartwright how she felt about him all the years of their lives. No, she'd wimped out and written him a letter confessing her feelings. He'd never responded. And then he'd gone missing.

Just thinking about him now Beth felt a burning in her heart for what it would never have. Her inner lip burned from biting down. All eyes remained on her, waiting for her response. In times like these, she did what she always did, she turned to the Lord.

"I'm reminded of 1 Corinthians 13:13 where it says that faith, hope, and love abide, but of those three, love is the greatest."

Nathalie's face lit up once again, likely assuming that Beth was championing her cause.

"However," Beth continued, "just because love is the greatest thing in the world, it doesn't mean you can ignore faith and hope. It's hard for faith to take root when you've planted doubts in someone's mind and heart. Ask yourself if you've done that with your parents."

Nathaniel looked far off. Beth knew she'd reached him as he nodded while pursing his lips.

Nathalie sighed and rolled her eyes. But she didn't argue Beth's point. It looked like Beth had gotten through to both of them.

"I think you should take some time to show your parents the truth of your commitment. Let their faith in you be restored. Give it some time to grow and hope that they will come around to see the path you both wish to take. But, no, I don't believe you can force it."

The two would-be newlyweds looked at each other. Nathaniel lifted a brow. Nathalie lowered her lashes and gave him a barely perceptible head nod.

Beth smiled, a real smile this time. These two were in sync. They knew each other. They would make it. They left the office hand in hand, walking at a more subdued pace toward their future.

"Have I told you how much I am looking forward to not only marrying you but sharing my duties with you?"

Walter brought her knuckles to his lips for a light kiss. When he gazed up at her, there was a brightness in his brown eyes, turning them more hazel than coffee. It was the bright look of love that shone from his eyes.

Beth knew the look because she'd seen it reflected back at her many a time when she'd looked into Reece Cartwright's clear blue eyes. She'd been only seeing her reflection. Reece had never looked at her that way. And he never would.

For weeks, she'd mourned the loss of her first love when he'd been declared missing in action by the military. Only to find out last month that Reece might be alive. Though that had brought her relief, she was still out of sorts.

She'd written Reece a letter three months ago; a letter confessing her love for him. He hadn't written back. He'd always written her faithfully be it over email or a handwritten note. But he'd gone silent after that revealing missive.

He might have never received it. Military mail could be delayed, especially when soldiers were deployed. Whether he'd received it or not, she hoped more than anything that he was still alive and would soon be found.

But for now, Beth had chosen to move on. She'd waited her whole life for Reece Cartwright to love her, and it was clear he did not.

She turned back to Walter, who was still waiting

for her response to his compliment. Beth reached out and grasped the hand of the man who reached for her. It felt good to be wanted. It felt warm. It didn't burn like rejection, or worse, silence.

"I'm looking forward to our life together too," she said.

CHAPTER THREE

He found a Polaroid. Four people smiled back at him. All four looked alike. Two older, two younger. A family.

The redheaded woman smiling back at him was only familiar because of her hair. There was a rosy blush to her high cheeks. Her smile was big; nearly as big as her face. Her green eyes were big and bright. She had the type of friendly face that made others feel it was safe to tell her their secrets.

She stayed frozen in that smile, as though someone had told her a joke. The punchline was captured forever in the celluloid. A happy moment frozen in time.

She wasn't alone in that moment. Next to the grinning redhead stood a gray-haired man. His eyes were big, but bushy brows took up most of the real estate. His pupils were small and beady, like a wise, old owl. But they were the clearest blue. The man had long limbs that rivaled the wingspan of an owl. He stood with one arm around the woman and the other around two other people in the frame.

The two younger people were carbon copies. A girl and a boy. They both had flaming red hair like the woman and bright blue eyes like the man. Siblings. Twins.

The boy possessed the face he'd seen reflected back in the mirror that morning. Reece was the man's name. Reece was *his* name. Private Reece Cartwright of the United States Army.

"How are you holding up?"

Reece looked up from the polaroid of his family. Cpl. Brandon Lucas looked down at him with concern. Everyone Reece had encountered the past two weeks that he'd been awake looked at him with concern.

He'd only seen the eyes of the women who had taken care of him in the cave. In just that sliver of a glimpse, and in the short amount of time he'd been conscious, he'd discerned a mountain of worry in their features. The endless stream of men and women in tan, brown, and green uniforms that had poked, prodded, and questioned him for days on end all wore pinched expressions when they regarded him.

Corporal Lucas had always been nearby. His worry had taken time to develop. The first thing Reece had gotten from the man was an overwhelming sense of relief. But now, two weeks later, his brow was perpetually wrinkled each time he looked Reece over.

"I'm fine." Reece knew he said the expected thing when Corporal Lucas nodded.

"You're not fine," said Brandon. "But what else could you say?"

Reece had been taken from the bombed out structure where he'd been hidden. Apparently, the women had protected him at great peril to themselves after he had tried to protect them from insurgents. Reece and his four-man fire team had been stationed in the area on a surveil and reconnaissance mission. They were tasked with gathering intel on some structures thought to be in use by an anti-coalition militia.

From what they could gather, Reece had seen the women headed toward the area. There was some uncertainty of whether the women were in the wrong place at the wrong time or if they were a part of the militia. Reece was the only member of the team who spoke the language. With his team covering him, he approached the women. And then fire rained down on all of them.

Reece remembered none of it. Only waking up. Even though the two weeks that he'd been awake were a blur. It was difficult for him to hold anything, especially names and faces. His mind felt like it was rebooting and installing a new systems update, all while crashing at the same time.

Reece pressed his thumbs to his temples. The move didn't offer much relief. The pain was inside his head. He needed a way to let it out.

He closed his eyes, shutting out the bright light of the day. That helped. Darkness was the only thing that soothed him. A large hand clapped down on his shoulder, causing him to wrench his eyes open.

"Don't stress yourself, Cartwright."

Corporal Lucas sat beside him in the moving vehicle. The worry was gone from the other man's gaze. In its place was certainty. Reece wished he felt some of that.

"The doctor said the amnesia is likely temporary," said Corporal Lucas. "It'll all come back when you're ready."

Reece dropped his hands from his temple. The

Polaroid was still on his lap. He looked again at the family, his family. They looked happy, without a care in the world other than the care for each other. He wished he could remember how to feel that way.

"You've been through a lot. We're all just glad to have you home."

Home. Reece was home. He looked out the window of the moving vehicle to see mountains and a blue sky. It looked somewhat like the valley that he'd been pulled out of. But the buildings were all erect and sturdy. Still, none of it looked familiar.

"Reegan is going to maul you when she sees you."

Reegan. His twin sister. Reece pressed his thumb and forefinger into the snapshot of the life he couldn't remember. He ached for something, anything familiar.

"She insisted you were still alive. She never gave up. She demanded we go back for you."

Reece felt gratitude toward the woman but still no familiarity. He reached for the duffle bag of his belongings and put the picture back inside. His fingers grazed a leather-bound book inside. He peered inside the dark bag and pulled out a small Devotional Bible.

The pages were worn. The spine broken. It

looked well used and well cared for. Was he a religious man?

He thumbed through the pages. Many of the corners were dog-eared. There were highlights in yellow, pink, and blue. The margins were filled with notes in black and blue ink. In the Book of John, with the highlighted verse about friendship, there was a letter. Before he unfolded the letter, Reece read the verse.

Greater love has no one than this, that he lay down his life for his friends. John 15:13.

That felt familiar. But even more familiar was the handwriting inside the letter. A spark of recognition hit him. He knew this handwriting. It was familiar.

A warmth spread through his chest as his gaze slid over the carefully written script. The T's all had loops. The L's slanted to the right. The small case S's had fat bellies that made them resemble hearts.

I need to tell you what's in my heart. I love you. I've always loved you.

Reece's first instinct was to put the letter away. He felt as though he were intruding. It was obviously a love note. Then he scanned up and saw his name at the top.

My dearest Reece.

It's easier to write to you than it is to speak to you.

We've been in each other's lives for so long, but my feelings for you have only deepened through the years. There has never been anyone else for me. There never will be. You are my best friend. I'd like to offer you my heart. I know that you care for me, but I'm asking if you could ever love me?

It was signed *Beth*.

Reece tried to picture Beth in his mind. He didn't get a face. But he did get a feeling. It was warm and cozy. Was that love? Did he love Beth?

He jolted forward as the truck came to a stop. The letter tumbled out of his hands, fluttering in the air. Reece caught it before it could hit the ground.

"We're here," said Corporal Lucas.

Whoever Beth was, and what she might be to him, Reece was about to find out.

CHAPTER FOUR

Beth frowned down at the rich earth below her. Part of her was happy for the plants thriving in such nutrient-dense soil. Another part of her knew that it wasn't just little seedlings ready to poke their heads out of the fertile ground.

An earthworm slithered between a rock causing her to gag. She cringed and shuddered when a beetle lumbered over a long blade of grass. Beth forced herself to lower the gardening spade and pray for patience and compassion for all God's creatures.

"You know it's more afraid of you than you're afraid of it."

Beth wasn't afraid. She was grossed out and uncomfortable and wishing for hardwood floors and air conditioning. Clearly, gardening wasn't her favorite activity. She didn't like getting dirty. The picnic blanket she knelt on kept her yellow dress from getting messy. She'd switched out of heels and changed into running shoes. Unfortunately, her nails would suffer the consequences of girl time.

Reegan Lucas's smile was brighter than the sun. The tan on Reegan's left hand showed a visible band line where the ring should go. Beth's best friend wore a diamond ring around her neck as she dug her bare hands into the dirt. Reegan had been married for just over a month. It clearly agreed with her.

A lovely hum rose as Reegan sang a hymn. The sound of her voice wafting on the light wind made butterflies flutter. Butterflies Beth could handle. It was the slimy baby caterpillars that made her skin crawl.

"Any word from Brandon?" asked Beth.

Reegan's smile fell a bit, but only slightly. "Not for two weeks."

Reegan's husband, Corporal Brandon Lucas, had been on the original mission where Reece had gone missing. When the army announced they were putting together a retrieval operation, he stepped up. Beth had gotten the sense that Brandon felt responsible for losing Reece. The honorable man that he was, she hadn't been surprised when he'd stepped up in the effort to get his fellow soldier back.

The cold metal of the gardening utensil wasn't what made Beth shiver. It was the thought of seeing Reece alive and breathing and fine. No matter how awkward things might be between them, she wanted that more than anything in the world. She'd had trouble fathoming a world where Reece wasn't in it. She would happily live in a world where he was alive and well, even if their friendship didn't survive.

"Brandon prepared for the mission," said Reegan. "And he prepared me. He said there was a possibility of three dark weeks where I wouldn't hear from him. So, it should be just another six more days, then I should hear something."

Six days. They'd know something in six days.

Beth placed her palms in the dirt, needing something solid and warm to quell the jitters shimmying over her skin. With her right hand, she cleared a path for the string beans struggling to take root. She pushed the white roots back into the earth to give them purchase with her left hand.

"Let's talk about something else," said Reegan. "Let's talk wedding plans."

Beth's shudders were replaced with a rumbling in her tummy.

"Mine was quick but still perfect. I got my dream man." Reegan pressed her hand to her ring over her heart.

Beth carefully averted her gaze from her best friend. If Reegan looked in her eyes, she might see that she was dreaming of another man. Her own engagement ring caught the light. The small, colorless rock felt heavy on her hand. That had to mean it would sink deep into the foundation and make sturdy roots.

"But it's the marriage that counts, not the wedding," Reegan continued. "Just know that since we have time to plan, I will be living out my dream wedding through yours."

It wouldn't be the wedding Beth had dreamed about. That dream had featured another man. Beth had never told Reegan about her infatuation with Reece. The three of them had been as thick as thieves since they were in the cradle. Both Reegan and Reece were her best friends. Since they were girls, Beth had relied on Reegan for all things boy band, fashion, and feelings.

Reece was more of an academic. He loved all things scholarly, especially when it came to scripture. He'd even taken to learning the ancient languages like Arabic and Hebrew, which was a prized skill in the military.

When they were younger, the two of them would talk well into the night on a myriad of Biblical and spiritual topics. Beth had cherished those times as some of the most enlightening moments and enriching experiences in her life. Reece had always made her feel heard and important. He just hadn't known he'd also made her feel something more, something in her heart.

"Have you two set a date yet?" said Reegan.

"Not yet. I was thinking winter."

Beth looked up at the mountains and the sunny skies. The bare branches were just beginning to sprout new leaves.

"Winter? That's months away," protested Reegan. "At least we'll have time to plan."

"Reegan, Walter is only a youth pastor. We're just going to do something small."

"You might think you're just going to do something small, but you're this town's favorite daughter. And, thanks to the Purple Heart Ranch and its zoning, this town hasn't had anything except quickie weddings in months."

When the soldiers had moved onto the ranch and

converted it into a place of rehabilitation for veterans, they hadn't read the fine print. A zoning regulation had stipulated that all permanent residents had to be families. That meant the men who'd been living there for a year and getting the much-needed care they required had to either fight through a wad of red tape or get married. Surprisingly, they all chose marriage.

"Beth?"

Beth looked up to Reegan, meeting her gaze for the first time that morning. There was concern in her best friend's clear blue gaze. Beth gasped a little. Sometimes it shook her how alike Reegan and Reece looked.

"Are you sure about this?" Reegan asked.

Beth set her mouth to assure her oldest friend, but her throat went dry. At the same time, she felt a desperate need to swallow down bile. Before she could give an answer, a golf cart pulled up with Private Mark Ortega behind the wheel. He hopped out of the cart looking very serious. His perpetual dimples were at ease today.

"Reegan, we need you to come to the medical center."

"Is something wrong?" Reegan asked as she stood, brushing the dirt from her hands.

Mark shook his head. But the corner of his lips tugged up, and his dimples gave it away.

"He's back," Reegan breathed.

The dimples went on full assault as Mark grinned his answer.

"And Reece?"

Mark's smile wavered, the dimples dimming.

Beth felt nauseous. Why a half smile? Either Reece was back. Or he wasn't. Or he was back but not alive.

"He's here," Mark confirmed.

Beth sagged down to the ground. Her fingers took root in the soil. Her rear came to the grass, staining her dress. She didn't care.

He was here. He was back. He was alive.

"Come on, Beth."

Beth looked up. Reegan was beckoning her into the cart. Neither her legs nor her hands would move. She'd taken root into the earth. A beetle crawled over her knuckles, and still, she didn't move.

"Beth, get in this car."

Beth shook the dirt and the bug off her hands. As she rose, she noted that her knees and the front of her dress had spots of dirt on them. On unsteady feet, she walked to the cart and slid in next to

Reegan. They held onto each other as the small, unwieldy cart rolled over the green pastures.

Beth wasn't ready to see Reece. It was enough to know that he was alive. But she knew she needed to see him, to confirm it. But also, that would be exactly what she needed to truly let go and move forward.

In no time, they pulled up to the medical building. Reegan leaped out, hitting the ground at a running pace. Beth's unathletic friend took the stairs three at a time and bounded through the glass doors.

Beth walked slowly up the stairs beside Mark. "Is he injured?"

"In a manner of speaking, yes." Mark took a deep breath in that way when someone had bad news to deliver. He let it all out in a gush. "He has amnesia."

Beth stopped in her tracks. She ran those three words over in her mind, again and again, making sure she understood them. Amnesia?

Reece had amnesia.

She said the words again and again in her head, as though she were trying to be certain that she remembered them.

Reece had amnesia.

That would mean he wouldn't remember anything. Including her. Including the letter.

As she came closer to the door, she heard the sounds of Reegan's sobs. And then she heard his voice.

"I'm sorry."

Beth stopped in her tracks. He sounded exactly like himself. His soft, deep voice reached her from the hall. She'd always marveled that someone with a resonant baritone could also speak so softly.

"It's okay," said Reegan. "I don't care that you don't remember. You're alive and whole. I remember everything. I can tell you your entire life story."

Beth stopped at the threshold. Reece sat in a chair. He wore a T-shirt and khakis, looking like his old self. His hair was cut close to his scalp as he preferred it. His chin was cleanly shaven. His bright blue eyes were clear, but there were bags beneath them.

He was smiling, but it didn't reach his eyes. He was thin and gaunt. He looked defeated and lost.

And then his gaze rose and found her. Beth braced herself for her heart to shatter when he didn't recognize her. Instead, she felt her heart sink. Not from breaking. It felt like a house settling into its foundation.

It didn't matter whether he remembered her or not. It didn't matter how long they spent apart. It didn't matter who came between them. She would always love this man.

She was thankful he wouldn't remember her letter. She was thankful he wouldn't know what would have never been. She could go on loving him in secret. And best of all, they could start anew and be just friends.

And then recognition lit his blue eyes. He reached out his hand. He reached out for her.

"Beth?"

CHAPTER FIVE

Reece had long lost count how many different rooms he'd been in over the past two weeks. It wasn't that he couldn't remember them all. His brain worked fine at recording the details of everything he encountered from the moment he opened his eyes back in that cave. It was just that he was too exhausted and disinterested to keep track of what was going on around him.

His disinterest extended to more than just the rooms. He hadn't made much effort to remember the multitude of names and faces that paraded around him. There was an endless sea of people. They moved in and out of his vision. They asked him the same questions over and over again. Over and over again, Reece gave the same answers; *he couldn't remember.*

He had tried at first. However, every time he got close to the light of old memories, a blinding pain seared his mind. The backs of his eyelids burned. The smell of smoke choked his throat. His palms sweated, and his legs began to bounce. The only salve was to retreat.

He knew that retreat was not in his character. He admitted to being a weakened man right now. He was no longer in physical pain. All aches had left him before he'd left the base in Afghanistan. He didn't have a single bruise on his body. But his mind was weary. And that's what was asked of him day in and out: *remember, think, consider.*

That light of remembrance was far too powerful in his present state. He knew he'd have to face it. But later.

Now he just wanted to shut his eyes. Shut them all out and get lost in the darkness. That was until he saw her …

Sergeant Chase—Colin, his superior had insisted Reece call him—had driven them into town from the airport. Reece had caught flashes of some memories from his time in this town. Having an ice cream at the shop with the pink trim. He knew there was a cozy spot in the library he preferred. He had the strongest reaction to the church that sat at the end of the main street. That place called to him as though it were a second home.

None of the town memories were painful. But trying to pull them closer to him, trying to delve deeper into the flashbacks, brought on the threat of the bright, hot light. He'd backed off, slunk down in the rear seat of the truck, and closed his eyes.

Corporal Lucas—Brandon, he'd insisted Reece call him—and Colin had let him rest in the car. Though Reece had no memories of either man, he trusted them both immediately.

Reece knew he liked the ranch nurse and doctor as well. The pretty, brown-skinned nurse named Ruhi took his vitals. She spoke like they knew each other, but she hadn't pressed him to remember.

An older, male version of her appeared in the door next. Reece knew it was Nurse Ruhi's father. The connection was clear. Reece had no visual memories of Dr. Patel either, but he felt at peace around the psychologist.

Dr. Patel hadn't asked questions about the mission or his memory. He asked questions about Reece's health and wellbeing. The doctor's voice was familiar to Reece. It was soft and calm like his words could have been a lullaby. Reece was content to simply listen while the man spoke.

Reece settled back in his chair, near lethargic after the long days of travel when a red-haired tornado nearly bowled him over. Her impact pushed the front two legs of the chair off the floor as she crashed into his chest. She squeezed the life out of him and drenched his shirt front with tears.

"I knew you were alive," she sobbed. "I felt it in our connection."

She pulled away from him, and Reece looked into his own blue eyes. In his mind, there were flashes of her smiling over at him. Flashes of her nostrils flaring at him in anger. He remembered the sound of her laughter. But even more, he remembered the sound of her voice singing. The lyrics were imperceptible, but he knew that he'd know her song anywhere.

"Reegan."

It was as though a lightbulb went off behind her eyes. "You remember me."

Reece winced. "I'm sorry."

Before he could let her down, she shook her head and squeezed his shoulder.

"It's okay," she said. Her smile was wobbly, but he could see her resolve. "I don't care that you don't remember. You're alive and whole. I remember everything. I can tell you your entire life story."

It felt right to hold her to him. He did feel a connection to her, though he didn't feel comfortable vocalizing it as she had. He had the overwhelming urge to apologize to her again. The apology caught in his throat when the vision in yellow appeared in the doorway.

She stood in a shard of light that should've made Reece cringe had it been anyone else. But he couldn't look away from her. She glanced around the room, but not at him. There was uncertainty in her hazel eyes. She bit at her lip, tugging it into her mouth as though she wanted to speak but was afraid. And then her gaze met his.

Reece felt like something kicked him in the chest. He was convinced his heart began beating for the first time. Before that moment, the organ had only been a murmur. He'd been breathing shallowly, but he took his first deep breath. He had no choice. His lungs needed to expand to fit the sudden growth of his heart.

Like with Reegan, Reece saw flashes of this woman from times past. He saw her smiling, laughing, indignant, compassionate.

He felt connected to her as well, an invisible

bond that felt all too real. Yet the bond he shared with her took a different route to his heart. A route that had been under construction and was now in the final stages of completion. When he spoke, the finishing touches were added.

"Beth?"

It wasn't a question. He knew it was her. She was the first thing he was certain of outside of his sister.

Beth's uncertain gaze went wide, like saucers filled with hope. Her lips shaped into a delicate O. Her fingers untangled and rubbed down her sides, smoothing the pleats of her skirt.

Reece felt parched watching her. The dress made her look like a young, fifties housewife. A vision of Donna Reed flitted through his mind. He remembered that he loved that show. That and another show about a boy named Beaver, but he couldn't recall the title. He didn't care to. His mind was wrapped around the vision in the doorway.

Beth was licking her lips again, in preparation to speak. Reece's gaze latched onto the motion. Had he ever kissed those lips? He wanted to fight the pain of the light to uncover one of those memories.

"You remember me?" asked Beth, her voice a shaky whisper.

Reece's gaze swept her body. Long brown

hair that brushed her shoulders. Long legs that ended in—running shoes? That didn't seem right.

He continued his perusal to her long slender fingers. On her left hand, on the fourth finger, there sat a sparkling diamond. And now Reece's lips parted in an O.

The letter. He must've answered her plea of love. Now he knew what his answer had been.

"Yes," he said.

Yes, he did remember her. As much as he remembered his sister. Just a feeling of familiarity. But it was too hard to explain.

Reece wasn't certain of the expression that crossed Beth's features. Surprise? Happiness? Horror? Resolve?

Had they fought the last time they spoke? Had they argued? She was still wearing his ring. So, whatever disagreement they may have had, they hadn't broken things off.

He glanced at the ring again. The jewelry didn't suit her. It was small and colorless. That seemed wrong. But perhaps it was all he could afford at the time?

"How is it he remembers Beth and not Reegan?" asked Brandon.

Dr. Patel shrugged. "The mind is fickle. He may be simply remembering what is comfortable."

"What?" said Reegan. "I make him uncomfortable?"

Reece ignored his sister. He knew she wasn't upset. He felt certain that the three of them had always been close. Instead, he focused his attention on Beth, particularly on her dress. He spotted smudges of dirt on the front and green stains on the side.

"I remember ..." Reece fought the wince. He wanted this memory to come through. He took a breath and began again. "I remember swinging on the monkey bars while you and my sister sat on the side. I jumped down to the ground. It had been raining earlier, and it was a bit muddy."

He glanced up at Beth. She hadn't taken a step over the threshold. Her hand was on the door frame as she watched him. Her knuckles were white as she gripped the frame.

"I got mud on your dress. You got very angry with me. You don't like to be dirty." He frowned at the mud on her dress and knees.

Beth looked down and brushed at the smudges on her dress. "I was helping Reegan weed in the garden just now."

Reece's gaze went to his sister. "Reegan loves gardening."

His sister's smile was brilliant and wide. She nodded her head vigorously. "I do. I love gardening."

"There's a garden out back of our house." Reece saw the patch of green out back of the red brick house. He felt an overwhelming nostalgia to be in that place. That place would be safe. "I'd like to go home."

CHAPTER SIX

As the others took a moment and explained the tragedy of the Cartwright home to Reece, Beth gripped the frame of the doorway. Her breaths came up short, which was a problem because her racing heart needed more oxygen to pump blood down to her weakening knees.

Reece remembered her.

Selective memories, true. But look at what he'd selected. He'd pulled out times from their childhood when things were innocent and pure. He remembered small things about her, like the fact that, unlike most kids, she didn't like to get her hands or her clothes dirty.

She didn't have the mental capacity to determine

whether this was a good thing or a bad thing. She simply gloried that it was a thing. She was important enough for his brain to hold onto as everything else went dark.

She'd always known she'd mattered to him. He'd told her many a time that her friendship meant the world to him. But now she knew that memories of her were a comfort, and that warm, cozy feeling of comfort was found in the heart.

He remembered the good things. He hadn't remembered the letter. He might not ever. That meant they could be friends again.

Beth tried to gulp down a deep breath, but her lungs didn't inflate all the way. There was a lot of empty space in her chest. It was as though her heart had shrunk down in disappointment.

Despair colored her vision. Her mouth went dry. The palms of her empty hands itched. She balled her hands into fists and met a sharp point on her left hand.

Common sense told Beth that it wasn't possible. Memories or not, she and Reece could never be the friends that they had been. She was still in love with him. And here she stood wearing another man's ring.

Reegan sat next to her brother. She took his hand in hers as she relayed the tragedy of the fire and the loss of all they held dear.

"Where will I stay?" Reece said.

"You'll stay with us," said his sister. "Here on the ranch. Now that you're here, we can rebuild the house, but it will take a while."

Reece frowned looking between his sister and her husband. Brandon stood behind Reegan's chair, just off to the right of her shoulder. He looked to Beth like a sentinel, ever watchful of a precious treasure.

"Aren't you two just married?" Reece asked. "No offense, but I'd rather not stay in the room next door to newlyweds."

Reegan's cheeks heated at her brother's words. Brandon cracked a grin.

"You could do what all the other soldiers did," Ruhi spoke up from her place next to the medical equipment. "You could get married. Then you could have your own home here on the ranch."

The nurse said it with a smile. It was likely meant to ease the tension that had clouded the room. But no one laughed.

Brandon's right brow lifted in consideration.

Reegan pursed her lips, the way she'd done in math class when puzzling over a particularly tricky problem. Pastor Patel smiled in that way when Beth would come to talk to him about an issue and come to a resolution without him ever offering any advice.

Beth's knees solidified at that moment. She pushed off the wall and took one step into the room. But she stopped before she could take another step.

She'd been about to raise a protest. The idea was ludicrous. Reece marry a stranger? Or worse, an ex-girlfriend.

Mindy Engle was still in town. She'd just gotten out of a long term relationship. Beth had seen her nursing her wounds a few times at the ice cream parlor last month.

The idea of Reece and Mindy back together? Forever this time? It was more than Beth could manage.

But she had no say. She couldn't even mount a credible argument. Not with the rock on her finger holding her back.

"That's not a bad idea."

The sound of Reece's voice had always sent a flood of warmth through Beth. Now it just delivered chills. An icy cold that made her shiver and want to jump into a fire.

"Unless I'm mistaken," Reece continued. "I believe I'm already engaged."

Now Beth wanted the fire to form a pit and bury her alive. So, she and Reegan weren't the only women he remembered. There was someone else. Someone else he loved and had proposed to.

"I only hope she'll still have me."

Whoever this girl was, she'd be a fool if she didn't. Reece Cartwright was an amazing man. The best man. The man of her dreams who she was never meant to have.

"Will you, Beth?"

There was a tingling in her chest. That was the first sign that she was still alive after being dealt a deathblow. When Beth lifted her head, she felt dizzy. Had she been holding her breath the whole time?

Her gaze locked on Reece. He'd asked her to do something for him. Was it something to do with the wedding? Did he want her to go and find Mindy? She'd die again if he asked her to have any part of this wedding.

"Will I what?" Beth's voice croaked like a toad when it finally bubbled past her constricted throat.

"Will you still have me as your husband?"

Everything and everyone in the room went still. There had been a fly buzzing on the window. It held perfectly still, as though it also couldn't believe what had just transpired.

Had Reece Cartwright just said what she thought he said? To her?

"Can we have a moment in private?" said Reece.

Slowly, everyone filed out. Ruhi mouthed *OMG* to Beth as she followed out her father. Brandon had to practically lift Reegan off her feet to get her moving. Even the fly followed the others out of the room.

Once the room cleared, Reece turned away from her. He looked down at something in his lap. It was his father's old Bible, the one he'd given to Reece when he'd gone off to college. Reece opened the well-loved pages and unfolded a piece of paper. Beth's heart kicked up again when she recognized her handwriting.

"I've been reading and rereading it. Your handwriting was the first familiar thing to me. I couldn't remember your face, but I knew that I cared for you. Every time you wrote the word *love,* I felt it in my soul."

Somehow, Beth made it over to the chair beside him. It was just in time because the next words out of his mouth would have sent her to the floor.

"I love you, don't I? We love each other?"

She had to be dreaming. This was how it always happened in her dreams. His blue eyes gazing at her, only brighter as the light of realization dawned in them. He always scanned her entire face as though seeing her anew, just like he was doing now.

"It's the first thing that felt real to me."

Reece took her hand. The left one. Beth nearly jerked her hand back when he found Walter's ring.

"I asked you to marry me, and you said yes, right?"

He frowned down at the ring, cocking his head and squinting like he knew it didn't belong.

"I guess this was all I could find out in the desert."

"It's not yours." Beth choked the words out. "I mean, it's not what I wanted."

He nodded. "I know. There's no color. You like colorful gems."

"Yes."

"I can get you a ring with every gem imaginable."

"Yes."

"I know I don't have all of my memories. I have no idea what I'll do to support you. But, Beth, you're the only thing I feel certain about. Will you still marry me?"

"Yes."

There was no hesitation. Beth took off the ring and set it aside. Then she did what she'd been dreaming of since she was a little girl. She threw her arms around the man she'd loved her whole life.

CHAPTER SEVEN

*D*arkness settled all around him like a warm blanket. He swathed himself in it, pulling it tighter over his head, tucking the sheets beneath his chin, curling the edges under his toes so that the blackness could not escape.

Reece knew that outside the large, downy comforter the sun had risen. For the first time since he'd awakened to darkness, he wanted to greet the day. He was finally looking forward to something. Or rather someone.

Beth.

He ripped the sheets from his person and instantly recoiled. Though his body was ready for the day, his mind wasn't. The bright light made him wince as it threatened him with visions he wasn't ready to see.

An explosion of light. Ear piercing screams. The salty taste of panic. The metallic smell of fear. And finally, darkness.

The darkness was the only safe place. He had to hide in the darkness. Not forever, just for a moment.

As he made to settle back under the thick sheet, a quick succession of taps sounded at the door. Reece hit the floor. He threw his arms over his head as his knees impacted the solid wood.

"Cartwright, open up. It's Ortega."

The sound wasn't gunfire. It was knocking. It wasn't an adversary. It was company.

Reece noted that he'd reached to his side, but there was no weapon. He didn't need a weapon. He wasn't in a combat zone. He was on a ranch in his hometown. He was safe.

Opening his eyes wide, he yanked on a pair of pants and a T-shirt. Padding out of the bedroom in the small row house, he went to the front door. He pulled it open to reveal a young man his age, dark hair, bright eyes, and twin dimples.

A flash of memory featuring those dimples snaked through Reece's mind. Women smiled and giggled all around Reece and Private Mark Ortega whenever he flashed those dimples. But then the scene changed. Ortega wasn't smiling anymore. His eyes were alert as he watched Reece put distance between them. There was worry on his brow. And then abject horror as the blinding bright light separated them.

Reece stepped back from the sunlight shining in the doorway.

"You good?" Ortega clamped a hand down on his shoulder.

Reece shrugged out of Ortega's hold. He shook his head, shaking the memory loose until it went back in the darkness. "Yeah, I'm good."

Ortega looked as though he wanted to ask more, but like Brandon and Sergeant Chase, he didn't. There seemed to be an unspoken code between the four men that they only shared what and when they were ready. Reece wasn't ready.

"I'm here to walk you over to Patel's office."

"I can remember where it is." Reece's expression was pinched as he stepped into a pair of running shoes at the door.

Ortega punched him in the shoulder, lightly, but enough for him to feel. "Don't think I'll take your attitude 'cause you got knocked in the head."

Reece laughed, closing the door and rubbing his

shoulder. The exchange felt familiar between the two men. He also appreciated that Ortega wasn't treating him with kid gloves like the others.

"You know you were up for a promotion," Ortega said as they walked the green path toward the medical offices. "You'll probably get it now. If you still want it. If you decide you want to go back."

"Go back?"

"Into the Army. Re-enlist. Though I hear you're thinking of a different title? Husband?"

Reece's mind went back to Beth. He was going to marry Beth. The idea of going back to the army held little appeal to him when placed beside that idea.

"Man, what is it about this place?" asked Ortega. "Single men drop like flies here. I need to get out of here soon."

Reece wasn't sure what the man was talking about. But confusion was a common enough occurrence with him these days. He decided to enjoy the crisp morning air and the stunning view of the mountains instead.

A few men were out riding horseback. A number of younger boys clustered around one of the barns looking up to a grown man with the countenance of a soldier and one prosthetic arm. A ragtag pack of dogs followed around a man with a long, angry scar on one side of his face.

With each step, Reece felt more and more at home. This was a place for people like him. People who'd been wounded by the ravages of combat and were now ready to heal.

They walked farther, and Ortega continued to chatter on. This seemed normal, as well. Ortega chattering on while Reece listened.

"So, you and the pastor's daughter?"

Reece frowned. "Beth is the pastor's daughter?"

Before Ortega could confirm, a memory came to Reece. He saw flashes of Beth; a young Beth in a bright green dress; a tall and gangly Beth in a slim pink dress with ruffles at the bottom of the skirt; and Beth as she was now in a stunning royal blue dress.

Each iteration of Beth in his mind had been standing beside a man at a pulpit. Reece couldn't see the man's face clearly. Still, he felt a deep connection to the man.

"Makes sense," Ortega was saying. "You were always a holy man with that Bible of yours. Always quoting verses and trying to help people find Jesus."

That sounded right. It sounded like the kind of man Reece wanted to be. Apparently, it was the kind of man he had been.

He felt a deep sense of trust in the Bible and in God. Though he couldn't remember much, he knew not to fear. He felt an unseen hand on his shoulder with every step.

"Look," said Ortega. "I'm sure you're not ready to remember a lot because of what happened back there. But when you are ..."

Ortega took a deep breath. He tilted his head up to the dawning sun. When he turned his gaze back to Reece, Reece felt an ominous foreboding.

"I want you to know when you're ready to hear about your sordid past ... don't trust me. I'll make it all up."

Reece laughed. He knew Ortega's words to be true. Mark Ortega had a serious side, but it was never the one he presented.

The two executed a complicated handshake. With another pat on the shoulder, Ortega took off. Reece made his way inside the medical building.

Instead of going into an exam room, he was shown to Dr. Patel's office. The ranch's resident psychologist smiled and rose when Reece came in.

"How are you feeling today?"

"Fine."

Dr. Patel's expression didn't shift a facial muscle

from its serene expression. Still, Reece got the picture that *fine* wasn't the right answer.

"You look rested," said Patel. "Nothing wrong with your sleep?"

Reece preferred to sleep. Even though he'd apparently been in a coma for days and then in and out of consciousness in the cave, he welcomed the dark oblivion sleep afforded. It was the bright light of his waking thoughts and the memories trying to invade that unsettled him.

"So, you and Beth?"

Reece blinked. The other doctors had launched into questions to get him to remember. Not this one. "Did you know us both before?"

Patel's smile brought to mind one of the many times Reece had climbed up on Santa's lap as a child. Jolly and expectant and ready to spread joy.

"I've known you both your whole lives," said Patel. "It was clear she adored you from a young age."

Now it was Reece's grin that felt ready to spread joy. It thrilled him that Beth's feelings had a long tail. He wondered when the first time he'd felt something for her was?

"It was always clear you cared for her, though your feelings were late to bloom."

Reece pursed his lips to know that. He didn't like the idea of Beth pining after him without him returning her feelings. But at some point, he'd come to his senses and asked for her hand.

"Do you remember proposing to her the first time?" asked Patel.

Reece shook his head. "She wrote to me, confessing her feelings. I still have the letter. I don't remember responding, but when I read the letter, I felt something, the first real thing I'd felt since waking up. And when I saw the ring on her finger—"

"The ring?"

"The engagement ring. That's when I knew I had proposed, and she'd said yes."

Dr. Patel nodded again. He wasn't smiling in serenity any longer. There was a slight tick on the left side of his face, as though he were chewing something over. He inhaled and let out a long breath.

"Is there something wrong?" asked Reece.

"No. Just realizing I'm going to need to clear my schedule for some individual and couple's therapy."

"Individual? You want to see us both separately?"

"It's fine."

Reece felt his shoulders snap to attention at the

F-bomb. It didn't sound truthful coming from the doctor's mouth.

"Really," smiled Patel. "It's nothing to concern yourself about."

"You don't agree with our engagement?"

"To the contrary, I've been pulling for the two of you for years. I've always thought you were a perfect match. We've all just been waiting on you. This is the right thing. It's just going to be painful for a minute."

"Because of my memory loss?"

"That, and other things. I won't worry you with that now. Now, we need to get you well both inside as well as out. We'll start with some EMDR treatments."

"What's that?"

"Eye Movement Desensitization and Reprocessing. It's a method where we manipulate the eyes to try and bring the left and right hemispheres of your brain into harmony so that you can recall events."

Reece winced. "Are you going to shine a light in my eye?"

"No. You just need to follow the movement of my finger."

"And that's going to fix me?"

"There's nothing wrong with you. Your memories are all there. You've simply locked them away."

Reece wondered if maybe his memories should stay locked away.

Dr. Patel sat back in his chair and folded his hands in front of him. Reece knew he hadn't said the words out loud, but he got the sense that Dr. Patel knew exactly what was on his mind.

"We'll start next week," Patel said. "Today, you'll do some occupational therapy."

"Do you mean something like taking apart and putting together a gun?"

"No, you're going to go and milk the cows."

CHAPTER EIGHT

"**A**re you sure?"

Reegan rubbed her palm up and down her bare shoulder. There was a light breeze outside, but they were inside the church hall where it was warm. It was the billionth time Reegan had asked Beth that question in the last twenty-four hours.

"Yes," Beth hissed. She didn't glance over at her best friend. Neither did she apologize for her short temper in the use of the single word. Beth knew Reegan would ask her again in another five minutes. The answer would be the same.

Yes, she was sure she was going to marry Reece. Yes, she was sure she was about to break up with her previous fiancé so that she could take on the suit of her new one.

Beth and Reegan sat outside the youth pastor's office. The door was closed, and a low murmur of voices wafted from the crack between the floor and the door frame. She didn't know who Walter was in there speaking with. She didn't knock to try and rush the conversation on. Although she was sure of the actions she was going to take when the door opened, she wasn't looking forward to having this conversation.

But she knew it was the right thing to do. She didn't love Walter. She might have grown to care deeply for him, but he would never have her heart. It had always belonged to Reece. It always would. And now, Reece wanted to accept it.

A quick pang went through Beth that Reece had only discovered he cared for her now that he couldn't remember anything else. But she shushed that fleeting feeling away.

This was all she'd ever wanted in her life; to be married to Reece Cartwright. She had no doubt that she'd make him happy. She knew more about him than he knew about himself. And that had even been true when he'd had his full faculties about him.

Beth would make him happy. This marriage would make her happy. Unfortunately, she'd have to hurt a good man to bring forth all the happiness.

The voices grew closer to the door frame. Walter and his guest were about to come out the other side. Beth gripped Reegan's hands. Thankfully, her best friend knew better than to ask if she were sure again.

The door cracked open to reveal Walter's jovial face. His smile spread when he saw her. Beth stood in greeting, letting Reegan's hand go and preparing to speak a hard truth.

She could do this. This was the easy part. The hard part would be telling her father.

The door to Walter's office opened wider. A second figure emerged. Beth came face to face with her father.

Behind her, Reegan swore, but only loud enough for Beth to hear. Beth prayed that if her best friend were about to be struck down for cursing in the house of the lord, that she go with her. Eternal damnation would be better than facing this present.

"There's the bride to be," said her father. "We were just talking about you."

Beth swallowed. Her stomach grumbled, not wanting to accept the bile collecting in her mouth.

"We were thinking of a fall date for the wedding,"

said Walter. He came up and planted a chaste kiss at her cheek. "What do you think?"

Beth opened her mouth, but nothing came out. Her throat had grown thick with saliva since her stomach was still in revolt.

"Hello, Reegan," said her father. "Any word from Corporal Lucas about your brother?"

Reegan had to clear her throat twice before her words were audible. "Yes. They found Reece. They brought him back yesterday."

Pastor Barrett opened his palms and looked skyward. "To God be the glory. That is wonderful news. When can we see him? Is he well?"

Before Reegan could answer, Pastor Barrett turned back to Walter. "I can't wait for you to meet Reece. He's the son I never had. You two will get along famously. Beth was like a second sister to him. You'll bring him over as soon as he's well enough, Reegan? And I suppose you can bring that husband of yours too."

Beth's father had not taken to Brandon when he and Reegan decided to marry so quickly. He believed in couple's counseling and taking the time to court. Or at least he used to. Walter and Beth had only been dating for a couple of months, and now her father wanted to push the wedding.

"Well, I'll leave you two love birds to talk," said Pastor Barrett.

"No, Dad." Beth's voice rang loud and clear. Her mouth was now dry; her heart was now racing. "Don't go. You should hear this too."

Beside her, Reegan turned to step away. Beth grabbed her best friend's hand and held on in a death grip. Reegan's sigh of resignation was only slightly louder than her curse a moment ago.

The hall was empty, which was good. Beth didn't want to go inside Walter's office where the four walls would trap her. She preferred to be in the hall so she could run if cowardliness took over her, which was very close to happening.

Now that she had both men's full attention, and her voice was in working order, and her lifelong friend was bolted to her side by Beth's one hand, she wasn't sure where to begin.

"Reece is home, and he's ill."

Yes, that was a good tactic. Show how charitable this decision she'd made was. No selfishness in it at all.

"He's going to need someone to care for him."

"Of course," said her father. "You know his church family will be here for him."

Beth nodded. This was a good start. But she had

no idea in which direction to continue the conversation. So, she just blurted it out. "I'm going to be the one to take care of him."

Her father's gaze glowed with paternal pride. "You are such a good soul. I have raised a truly giving and wonderful young woman here, Walter."

"That you have, sir. I'm a lucky man."

Beth cringed. She was making this worse. Beside her, Reegan tried to wiggle out of her hold. Beth turned and glared at her friend until she held still. Reegan's shoulders slumped in complete surrender, and she stopped wiggling.

Beth decided the best way to get to the point was to bulldoze a path forward. She turned to Walter. "I can't marry you. I'm going to marry Reece."

Both men's reactions were twin mirrors. They both widened their gazes as they considered her words. Then their brows frowned as though they were repeating her statement over again in their minds for clarity. Then each of their heads snapped up as realization dawned at the exact same moment.

"I'm sorry." Beth handed over the pale engagement ring. "I've loved Reece my whole life. I tried to get past it, but I see now that I never will. It would be unfair to you, Walter. You are so good and kind. You deserve someone who will love you with all her heart, and that's not me because my heart belongs to someone else."

Beth sat the ring in the palm of his hand. She could've sworn she heard a thunk as the band landed on soft flesh. The rock was heavy, and it would make a good foundation, just not for her.

Walter looked hurt and shocked and confused. Beth's heart ached as she took one last look at him, but she knew it was the right thing to do. She could've never made him happy, not truly.

She turned to her father. The look of disapproval on his face made her want to sink into the ground. "I'm sorry, Daddy."

"Reece is a good man," said Pastor Barrett. "He would never take another man's fiancée. Did you tell him you're engaged to someone else?"

"I ..."

Her father's head lifted until he was looking down his nose at her in total censure. "You're making a mistake."

"No." Beth shook her head; the certainty she'd felt before the door opened returning. "I'm not."

Holding Reegan's hand tight, Beth turned on her heel and walked down the hall.

CHAPTER NINE

"Hmmm." There was surprise in that rumble that had a moment ago been doubtful. "It looks like you know what you're doing there."

Of course, Reece knew what he was doing. He'd grown up in Montana, not some concrete jungle. He'd milked his fair share of cows in his lifetime.

Reece was surprised he knew that about himself. General memories were easy. It was the specific ones that hemmed him up. Those memories were still shaky, coming in wisps. But his motor actions were fine.

They'd put the cow in a head catch. Reece knew he hadn't needed the assistance of such a contraption since he'd been a boy. Though he couldn't remember the first time he'd actually performed this specific task, he knew what he was doing.

Reece sat on a wooden stool. Using his booted toe, he slid the tin bucket beneath the cow's udder. He firmly grasped the animal's teat and got an annoyed moo from the old girl.

Okay, so he was a bit out of practice. He gentled his touch and began again. Making a ring with his thumb and index finger, he tightened his pointer finger in and brought each finger towards his palm one by one. The creamy substance flowed with ease into the bucket.

It was just like riding a bike.

Hmm? He wondered if he'd remember how to ride a bike. He certainly knew what one was.

"Your talk with Patel go well?" asked Dylan Banks.

Now that the man was certain his cow wasn't in jeopardy, his stance had relaxed. Reece hadn't recognized Dylan when he'd met the man. That was because they'd only met once before in passing, but Dylan knew his sister. Reegan had spent a lot of time at the ranch in the last year tending to the gardens.

"Yeah, it went well," Reece said.

"Did he go on about healing your inside as well as your outside?"

"Yeah, he did."

Dylan had smirked when he said it. The truth was, Reece was actually more interested in healing his heart. Unlike Dylan, who was missing a leg, Reece's limbs and extremities were fine. Reece knew he needed to recover what he'd lost. Still, a large part of him wanted to ignore the light trying to break through in his mind and instead focus on his heart.

"Listen to him," said Dylan. "His tactics may sound crazy, but he's usually right. Some of us believe he has a direct line to the man upstairs." Dylan pointed up to the heavens. "Anyway, I'll leave you to it."

Reece watched him walk off. He was left alone with only himself, the cow, and the bucket. Reece didn't prefer the solitude. But he also craved it.

Since he'd been awake, every person he'd encountered looked at him with expectancy. He knew they all were waiting for his memories to return. Reece felt certain that the memories would come back if he'd let them. But that would mean letting in that blinding, glaring light, and he just wasn't ready to face that pain.

The sun was up high in the sky. Reece used the

cow's body to shield himself from the rays. But the cow stepped back, and a shard of light pierced his eye.

Reece turned his face away, only to meet with another ray. He couldn't block out the memory that surfaced. It hit him square in the chest.

He heard the sound of a woman wailing. He couldn't see her face, but he recognized her voice. Looking back at the memory, he recognized the woman. She had been in the cave with him. She had stood in front of him when he was rescued.

Back in the memory, Reece felt his heart pumping. He felt his legs moving fast, hitting the pavement. The woman's eyes grew wider; her wails louder. Reece's arms came around her and then blinding red hot light. Then pain, blinding pain.

"Reece?"

His initial reaction was to jump, to jerk away, to put his hands up and ward off the intruder. But the sound of her voice, the touch of her hand, it was all a salve to his soul. Beth's hand rested on his shoulder. Her body blocked out the sun. The light and pain evaporated like a reverse tornado swallowing it all whole.

Reece opened his eyes wider to look upon his salvation. The shards of sunlight surrounding Beth were muted, but they were still there. The encroaching memories weren't done with him.

Beth's face went hazy before his eyes. Another memory came clearly into focus in his mind. But not of deserts and explosions. Instead, Reece saw her face.

A young Beth smiled up at him with adoration in her eyes. Another flash and it was her face again, only a few years older. She threw her head back and laughed. The sight made him catch his breath, the sound was a sweet tune. Then another flash a few years later. This time she looked at him with a softness in her gaze that Reece immediately recognized as love.

Beth Barrett loved him. Of that, he was sure. It was how she was looking at him now, once his vision had cleared and he was seeing the present moment.

Why hadn't he married her the first time she'd looked at him that way? What had taken him so long?

"Reece? Is everything okay?"

Reece pulled Beth to him. She was standing, and he was still on the stool. He didn't dare rise. He knew his legs would be shakier than a newborn calf after the assault inside his mind.

Beth came to him willingly, allowing his head to

rest against her chest. The closeness thrilled him, and he tightened his hold. He pulled her out of the light, turning her around so that his back was to the light. He would not let it consume her.

She put her arms around him. Her fingertips were a balm on his hot skin. "It's all right," she said.

And it was. So long as she was near, everything was all right. Reece wanted her like this in his arms every day.

He lifted his head and looked up into her bright eyes. Her lips parted on a gasp as she regarded him. He reached up and brushed a strand of hair from her face, tucking it behind her ear. Her hair was like spun silk. He could spend his days touching it, resting his nose in it, running his fingers through it.

His gaze traveled back to her lips. He willed a memory to come to him of kissing her. But his mind was dark now that he was turned from the light. Only she filled his gaze.

Had they kissed before? His brain hurt from the effort to wrangle free a specific memory of the feel of his lips against hers, the taste of her tongue, or the heat of her breath.

It was no matter. He could make new memories. Starting now.

Standing, Reece snaked his hand around the

nape of Beth's neck. The corners of her eyes widened, like a bird spreading its wings and preparing for its first flight. There was no resistance as he tugged her to him. She was a willing traveler on this journey.

Before he could touch her lips, the cow mooed. And then he heard a crash. The milk he'd gathered spilled over and onto the floor.

"I'm sorry," Beth said. As she'd stepped closer to him, her foot had caught on the pail. "I've made a mess of things."

Her hands went to her cheeks. Reece took a hard look at her then. He noticed the puffiness of her eyes. "Have you been crying?"

She shut her eyes. But that did nothing to hide the evidence. In fact, it only accentuated it.

"What's wrong? Tell me. I can't stand to see you upset."

Beth took a deep breath. When her gaze found him again, her smile wasn't bright. But there was a light coming from within. A light Reece wanted to bathe in for the rest of his days.

"I'm happy, Reece. I promise you. I'm just overwhelmed. I never thought I'd see this day."

"Because I went missing?"

She tugged her lower lip into her mouth. Her

head tilted a little to the left, like a newborn bird considering the distance from its nest up high and the unknown world down below. Finally, she gave Reece a curt nod.

Reece brought her into his arms. He towered over her. If she rested her head against him, it would fit right over his heart.

"I made my way back to you," he said. "Now we can pick up where we left off."

She rested her head against his chest, nodding vigorously. "We're going to make new memories."

"Not just new memories." Reece tilted up her face, so that he could see her eyes, but also so that he might take his first taste of her lips. "I also want to remember everything about you."

He bent to kiss her again, but she turned away. Twisting out of his hold and heading for the doorway where the sun was high in the sky.

"Have you had lunch?" she asked. "We should go and join everyone. We have a lot of planning to do for the wedding."

"All right." Reece winced at the light, but he didn't hesitate to join her. This woman was his past as well as his future. With her hand in his, he was certain he could face the glare of each new day.

CHAPTER TEN

Rain poured down in buckets outside. Not the pitter patter of an April shower. Literal buckets as if the downpour were coming out of a fireman's hose turned on full blast. The deluge had been going on for the last three days, not letting up for a split second. And now it was Beth's wedding day.

That was supposed to be a sign of good luck, right? Rain on the day of the wedding? Beth doubted it. She was sure someone made up the old wives' tale to make the bride feel better about the one thing out of her control on her big day; the weather.

Every bride who'd gotten married on the Purple Heart Ranch so far had done the ceremony outside. Beth would be the first forced into the barn. And that was after all of her guests would get drenched running from the muddy parking lot and into the damp, hay-strewn barn.

It wasn't just the weather that wasn't cooperating. Nothing else was going right. She'd stepped into her mother's vintage wedding dress, the dress she'd dreamed of wearing since she was a girl and her mother had shown her the beaded gown in the back of her closet. It was finally Beth's day to unzip the garment from its protective bag.

Even after twenty-five years of being in the back of a closet, the dress hadn't lost its luster. It was as pearly, pure white as the day her mother had said I do. The fit was perfect on Beth's figure. Unfortunately, when she tugged at the zipper on the side of the dress, the metal clasp broke.

"Don't worry," said Sarai Cannon. "I can fix this."

Beth didn't doubt that the former model could work her magic on the dress. What she couldn't help wonder about was what the next catastrophe would be?

Would the food get ruined? Would the sound system short circuit? Would Pastor Patel change his mind and not marry them?

Beth had always dreamed of being married by her father. However, the two hadn't talked since Beth had walked out of the church after announcing that her engagement to Walter was off.

She hadn't called her father either. She was far too frightened of his rejection than anything else. She knew that Pastor Patel, one of her father's oldest friends, had spoken to him. Pastor Patel had looked glum when he'd returned from that visit. Her father hadn't extended his blessing on the union, but neither had he barred his friend from performing the rights.

Beth had hesitated when she'd received the news. Her father was not a stubborn man. He always gave an ear to reason. Except when it came to his girls; and that included Reegan.

Pastor Barrett hadn't approved of Reegan's hasty marriage either. But eventually, he'd come around. That eventuality had happened on Reegan's wedding day when the man who had been a second father her whole life had shown up and walked Reegan down the aisle.

It wasn't too late. Her father might still arrive to perform that honor. There was a rustle outside the door. Beth held her breath as she waited for the person on the other side to present himself.

The door to the house opened. Instead of the familiar broad shoulders of her father, she saw the smaller frame of her best friend. Reegan ushered herself inside, tossing an umbrella back out the door. A gush of rain came in after her. Beth looked at her friend, expectantly. Reegan caught her glance and shook her head.

Beth's head dipped. Her heart sank. Her father wasn't in attendance. He wasn't coming. Not even to walk her down the aisle.

Outside, the rain beat a vicious pattern. It showed no signs of letting up. Beth straightened her shoulders. She was still going through with her wedding.

The one thing she knew for sure was that she loved Reece Cartwright. She always had, and she always would. Nothing would change that.

Especially now that she knew Reece wanted her too. He'd almost kissed her. She'd wanted that kiss more than she wanted this marriage. She'd turned away from him at the last second because there was one thing she wanted more than the marriage and the kiss. Beth wanted everything to be real with Reece.

So long as he had amnesia, they were living in a fantasy world and not reality. He didn't remember her, not really. He only had snippets of the whole. Tiny shards in a broken mirror. Beth wasn't sure if it was an adequate reflection of who she truly was, of who they truly were to each other.

At the same time, when she'd looked in his eyes these last few days, she'd seen something she'd only dreamed. Reece had always cared for her, of that she had no doubt. When he looked at her now, that affectionate glance held a spark of heat in its depths.

Reece Cartwright wanted her.

Beth knew that look well because she wanted him too. She knew that no one else would ever love him the way she did. She knew that no one else would care for him the way she could. That's why she would walk to him down that aisle. Come what may, memories or not, her feelings about him would not change.

This was the right thing. She didn't doubt that. She just wanted Reece, the old Reece, to know it for certain too.

"You're ready to go," said Sarai. The words were mumbled as she had a needle between her lips. Her fingers tugged up the zipper to the dress, closing Beth in and sealing her fate.

Beth looked at herself in the mirror. She took her own breath away. The beading of the dress sparkled back at her. The boning in the corset did wonders to her figure. She didn't look like herself. She looked like the woman she'd always dreamed of being on this day.

There was just one more piece to complete the look. The shoes. Beth stepped into her heels ... and the right stem broke.

Gasps rang up through the room. No sooner than the breath left every woman, did they each charge into action. They were all military wives, after all.

Maggie went looking for more shoes, only to discover that they were all too small or too large for Beth's feet. Sarai took the heel and attempted to glue the stem back on. Reegan pulled out the tennis shoes Beth often wore when she came to sit beside her friend in the garden, which turned out to be the winning solution. The dress was long enough to cover them.

Luckily, the laces didn't snap, and she didn't poke her toe out of the fabric. But Beth was done with holding her breath. She was done with the preparations. She just wanted to get to Reece before the next catastrophe befell her.

And so with her reconstructed zipper, and her flat, rubber shoes, she made her way over to the door. She turned the knob, girding herself for the downpour. The first thing that greeted her was sunshine.

The clouds were rapidly clearing in the sky. The sun's rays were stretching through the white wisps, as though waking from a leisurely afternoon catnap. But nothing compared to the bright bit of splendor that was the man walking toward her.

Reece was dressed in his Army uniform. His hair combed back, his chin clean-shaven. Despite the nightmares of the day, it was another of Beth's dreams come true.

This was exactly how she'd pictured it all these years. Reece would walk toward her, a slight smile on his face. Then he'd take her in, and he'd stop, just as he was doing right now. His gaze would sweep over her, and his blue eyes would light with fire, like the inner flame of a stovetop burner. That was happening too.

The only thing that was out of place in this real life fantasy was the umbrella in his hand. In her dreams, he always had a colorful bouquet of flowers. And sometimes there was ice cream in the other hand.

He held the umbrella up lamely as he spoke. "I know you don't like to get dirty. But it looks like we won't need this any longer." He tossed the device to the side. "Are you ready?"

He held out his arm. Beth came down the stairs and took the proffered limb. The sun broke through the clouds now, shining down on them. Looking up, the saw the colorful strands of a rainbow in the sky.

"It's beautiful," Beth said.

"It's fitting," said Reece. "The only way that rainbow could shine is after such a violent storm."

CHAPTER ELEVEN

Her skin hadn't come into direct contact with his, but Reece felt a cool heat where Beth rested her hand in the crook of his elbow. They'd shared a few light touches over the past couple of days that led up to their wedding day. But they hadn't been alone again. They were always surrounded by others. And in the few, brief moments when they were alone, Beth demurred.

He might not remember much, but he was starting to doubt they'd ever kissed. He now believed their courtship had been entirely through letters. He hadn't asked Beth for confirmation. It didn't matter because he knew she wanted him.

He knew that each glance she slid his way was full of longing. He saw her breath catch each time his skin faintly brushed hers. She would always linger a few more moments when it was time for them to part and go their separate ways. However, if he leaned in, if he gazed too long, she became flustered. So, he'd kept a respectable distance.

They were standing on the threshold of the barn doors. Once they crossed inside, they'd begin their wedding ceremony. He didn't feel a moment's hesitation about that. He knew in his soul that this was the thing he was meant to do, to be Beth's husband. To stand beside her and protect her for the rest of their days. He may have never kissed this woman, he may have never embraced her the way a man takes the woman whose heart he's been entrusted with, but he was certain he'd spend his life doing just that.

Looking down at Beth, he saw the brightness of love in her eyes. She looked at him with trust and adoration. He might not be certain of much in this unfamiliar life, but of that, he was sure.

Neither of their steps faltered as they approached the barn doors. Inside the large room, Reece saw a sea of unfamiliar faces. They all turned to look at the bride and groom. That's when Reece did stop, pulling Beth up short beside him.

"Where's your father?" He knew the groom wasn't

meant to walk the bride down the aisle. That honor was reserved for the father of the bride.

Beth's fingers trembled in the crook of Reece's arm. The sun shone down on her, but a cloud passed over her beautiful features.

"He's not coming." Her voice was small, her gaze downcast.

Her father wasn't coming? That didn't sound right. Reece knew that Beth's father doted on her. This, her wedding day, was not an occasion the man would miss.

"Is he ill? Should we postpone?"

Come to think of it, Reece realized he hadn't seen Pastor Barrett at all the last few days. He couldn't bring the man's face into view, but he knew he'd know him the moment he saw him.

Beth sniffed. Tears pooled at the corner of her right eye as she stared down at her hands. "He doesn't think we should get married."

Again, that didn't feel right to Reece. He couldn't pull up any specific memories, but he knew that Pastor Barrett loved him. Like a son.

With supreme gentleness, Reece put his forefinger under his bride's chin and lifted her face to meet his gaze. Their voices were hushed as they stood just outside the barn doors. Even more people had turned in their seats to stare. Reece ignored them all.

"Did I do something wrong?" Reece asked. "Is he angry with me?"

The clouds fled from Beth's features to be replaced with care and compassion. "Oh, no. Not at all. You didn't do anything wrong."

"Then, why?"

She took a deep breath. Then seemed to have trouble swallowing. "My father wanted me to marry someone else."

The thought of Beth and someone else lit a fire in Reece. The flame wasn't warm. It burned.

"The problem is that," she continued, "I've only ever loved you."

And just like that, the flame was extinguished with her words. Reece looked down at her, this woman who was pledging herself to him. Her lips were there for the taking. She wasn't demurring now. Her gaze slid to his lips in turn. She did not pull away. She did not turn away. Before he could take what she was offering, Reece had to make something clear.

"This might not sound genuine," he said, "because I don't remember everything about us. But I feel certain of this. I feel certain of us."

"Oh, Reece …"

The tears that had gathered at the mention of her father's absence collected more moisture. In another second, they poured down like the rains from earlier. Reece caught each and every one of them.

Beth's lower lip trembled as she looked up at him. He tilted her chin up. Her lips parted on a shaky exhale. The taste of her warm breath filled Reece with a mighty hunger.

He dipped his head for his first taste of this woman when a throat cleared in the distance. There was also a chorus of feminine sighs. An ensemble of masculine chuckles. And a few gleefully delivered *ewwws* by giggling adolescents.

The throat clearing is what both Reece and Beth heeded. Breaking apart, the two turned to face Dr. Patel, who was waiting for them at the end of the aisle. The man's lips were pursed, but there was an amused smile in the pinched expression.

"Sorry," Reece called to Dr. Patel.

"You're doing just fine on your own," he called from his place at the makeshift altar. "I couldn't do it better myself. But since my words will make it official, why don't you two come down here, and we'll get started."

Reece escorted Beth down the aisle. He looked to the right and left at the people gazing back at him. Everyone was smiling in approval at the two of them. A few handkerchiefs were pressed to eyes. Many hands were on hearts. A few of the soldiers held thumbs and fists up in the air.

In the features of every other face, Reece caught snatches of familiarity. The prickles of light began to overwhelm him. He turned away from the townsfolk and focused his gaze on Beth.

"I bless this union," Dr. Patel began, "because I know each of your hearts. Doubts will come into the light. Remember who you are and how you feel about each other when the light of truth gets too harsh."

The pastor tore his gaze from the couple and looked over their heads to address those gathered.

"God brought Reece back to us. Beth was the guiding light that brought him home. Their love was born in friendship, blossomed with time and maturity. This community has watched these two grow, and we will continue to nurture them and invest in their progress."

A chorus of *amens* rang through the barn rafters; the promises of a tight-knit community that Reece felt a connection to, even though he couldn't discern the individual threads.

"And now for the vows." Dr. Patel turned to Beth. "Repeat after me."

"In the presence of these, our family and friends, I, Elsbeth Elaine Barrett, do take you, Reece Joseph Cartwright, to be my husband, my partner, and friend. To join my life with yours, to share with you all that is to be, to laugh with you in joy, to comfort you in sorrow, to grow with you in love. I will honor you, I will be faithful to you, all the days of my life. This is my sacred vow."

Reece's fingers tightened around Beth's as she gave him her vow. When he was instructed, he slid the ring on her finger. She gasped at the perfect blue stone surrounded by a tiny sapphire, emerald, and ruby. When she looked up at him, her eyes shone with more tears.

Reece didn't have time to catch those ones. They would have to fall. It was time to give his own vow to the woman who'd indeed brought him back to life.

"With all my heart, I, Reece Joseph Cartwright, take you, Elsbeth Elaine Barrett, to be my wife. I promise to be your lover, your companion, and your friend. I will be your partner in joy, your ally in conflict, your greatest fan in all that you endeavor. I will be your comrade in adventure, your comfort in disappointment, your accomplice in mischief, your strength in times of need. I will listen with understanding and trust you completely for all the days of my life. This is my sacred vow."

Both Beth and Reece had allowed the elderly pastor to pick out their vows for them. As the other married couples on the ranch had informed them, the man had a way with vows. Each oath he swore made an imprint on Reece's heart as a solemn truth that he would defend for all his days.

"You may now kiss your bride."

Reece didn't need to be told twice. He gathered Beth to him, wrapping one hand around her waist and the other around the nape of her neck.

Beth took in a breath as she tilted her head back, opening for him. Reece brushed his lips lightly over hers. That first touch was like a match. The second touch caught fire. He ached to deepen the kiss, but the applause and shouts from the audience pulled him back.

That was their first kiss as husband and wife. It was the first kiss that he would remember. And it certainly wouldn't be the last.

CHAPTER TWELVE

The vows solidified it for Beth. This was definitely the right thing to do. Reece's words still echoed in her ears. It didn't matter that they were composed by another man. Pastor Patel had a knack for writing the vows of the ones he married. He always got to the heart of what the two people needed in their lives and crafted just the right words both needed to say to convey that.

She was Mrs. Reece Cartwright. All the doodling in her notebooks, all the pining each night in her childhood bed, all the wishing on stars falling from the skies, and pennies being tossed into wells, and prayers to God had manifested this.

Beth knew that when Reece said those vows, he'd meant them. If she hadn't believed his promises, then she would've known this was the right thing by that kiss. Oh, Lord in Heaven, that kiss.

The first brush of his lips against hers had been cursory. But the second taste had been filled with hunger. She knew because she'd felt it too. She'd wanted a third and fourth taste, but they weren't alone. They were in a room full of their closest family and friends. So, it would have to wait.

Until tonight.

Her wedding night.

Beth stumbled at the thought. Reece was there to catch her before she fell. They were making their way back down the aisle surrounded by the cheers and well-wishes of everyone they knew.

With her stumble, Reece looked at her with concern in his blue eyes. When he gathered that she was all right, he smiled at her. All worry about the night and what it held fled Beth's body to be replaced by the heat of desire.

As much as she'd dreamed of saying *I do* to Reece, she hadn't thought much about the wedding night. She'd been a girl with a crush. Then a woman with a broken heart. Now that she was Mrs. Reece Cartwright, her wedding night with her husband was all she could think about.

People came up and congratulated her, but all

Beth could think was whether or not they knew what the blush on her cheeks really meant. Food was passed around the table during the reception, but Beth couldn't eat a thing as she worried how the extra slice of bread might make her look later.

She watched Reece as he piled mac and cheese on his plate. Then greens. And, finally BBQ chicken. She wondered if he would mix them up like he did when they were younger.

As Mr. and Mrs. Fowler came over to offer their congratulations, Reece absentmindedly mixed the three dishes on his plate. He waited to take a bite until after the couple had moved back to their table. As Reece chewed his food, a look of pure ecstasy came across his features.

"This is my favorite, isn't it?"

He asked no one in particular. He was remembering more and more. What would happen when he remembered everything? And that everything hadn't included the love he'd professed for her today?

But she hadn't made this all up. He did feel something for her now. Which had to mean he'd felt something for her always. Love didn't just happen out of thin air. Right?

Beth wasn't sure. What she did know was that

now that she had his love, she wasn't going to give it up. She was determined to make her husband see that the love between them should've always been there.

"I know this song," Reece said.

The sappy love song blaring on the speakers had been the theme song at their junior prom. Her date, Steve Hudson, had gone off to kiss another girl midway through the dance when Beth hadn't offered her lips to him. Beth had been left standing alone on the dance floor. Until Reece came to her rescue.

Reece had come over to dance with her, even though he had brought Lisa Webber to the dance. This was the song that had been playing during that dance. Beth had listened to it on repeat for an entire year after the dance.

"Would you like to dance?" Reece asked her now.

Beth placed her hand in his. The colorful gems of her ring sparkled next to the gold band on his left hand. Reece led her out onto the dance floor. Wrapping his arms around her and holding her closer than he had when they were teens, he moved in time to the beat.

A few bars into the song and Beth began to wonder if he was remembering more than he let on. His steps anticipated the changes in the music where he could turn her, much like he did when they were at the school dance. Near the end of the song, he hummed a few of the lyrics. She'd heard the lyrics of unrequited love so many times, but never in the voice of the man she loved. Now that she had, the original version would pale in comparison.

Just before the song was over, Reece stopped. His steps halted, but he did not let her go. He pulled her close. But he wasn't looking down at her, he was looking away.

Beth turned to look over her shoulder, trying to see what had caught his attention. She knew it wasn't dangerous, as no other soldier was on alert. And she was right. There was no danger. Still, her heart skipped a couple of beats as the man approached them.

A broad smile crossed Reece's features as her father came up to them. Reece released his hold on Beth and opened his arms to embrace her father. "Pastor Barrett."

Beth's father looked surprised. His body stiffened, but he allowed the hug. After only a couple of seconds, all stiffness and stoicism went out of the older man. He lifted his arms and wrapped Reece in a firm grip, holding on a second longer.

Pastor Barrett pulled away and stared into

Reece's eyes. He began to say something and then choked up. Instead of trying to force the words, the older man hugged Reece to him again.

"I recognized you instantly," said Reece. "Just like I did with Reegan and Beth. I suppose that happens with the people I was closest too."

"It's good to have you home, son," said Pastor Barrett.

"I'm glad you made it," said Reece. "I know this was sudden, and I can't remember if I asked for your permission before I lost my memory, but know I'll cherish your daughter all my days."

Once again, the senior pastor of the church, the man who was never at a loss for words, choked on whatever he was about to say. Pastor Barrett took a deep breath and said his piece slowly.

"I practically raised you, so I know what kind of man you are. I couldn't want better for my daughter. You have my blessing. You always did."

And then father turned to daughter. Beth took a deep breath as her father regarded her. Even though it was her wedding day, she felt that she was about to be sent to time out for disobedience.

"May I have this dance?"

Beth let out the air she'd been holding. She literally flew into her father's arms. When he wrapped his arms around her, she buried her face in his chest and cried.

"I'm sorry, Daddy."

"I'm sorry I missed your vows. By the time I came to my senses, the ceremony had already started."

"You're here now."

"I am. I may not have agreed with how you got here, but I had always hoped that Reece would be your path."

"You did?" Beth glanced up at the man she respected more than any other in the world.

"Of course, I did." Her father brushed away the tears on her cheeks. "I know Reece would never hurt you."

"He's already made me so happy. And I'm going to make him happy, whether he gets his memories back or not."

"Then, you have my blessing."

The moment he said the words, Beth realized how much she'd needed to hear them. Now this, her marriage, her future, it all felt real.

CHAPTER THIRTEEN

The wedding festivities lasted far after the sun went down. Young and old continued to sway to the beats coming from the speakers. Plates and cups were refilled a few more times. Boisterous laughter could be heard from each nook and cranny of the enclosed yard just outside the barn.

Reece listened politely as unfamiliar faces came to tell him stories from his past. Stories he had no recollection of unless they featured Beth. If they brought up his wife's name, Reece would often get a sliver of vision of times gone by.

He'd reach out and try to touch those memories. He tried to pull the delicate strands closer. He wanted to hold onto anything that reminded him of her, his wife.

At times when his neighbors and friends brought up his parents, Reece looked away from the brightness of those flashbacks. The recollections didn't hurt like trying to remember the explosion back in the desert. Still, Reece knew that if he shone a light on those memories featuring his parents, those soft spots of light would only invite more glaring rays.

So, he listened politely without letting anything penetrate. Except, of course, for the times when someone mentioned Beth's name.

A next-door neighbor recounted the time when an adolescent Beth was bundled up in a parka out in her front yard. Apparently, Reece had come over to her, plopped down in the snow without his winter coat. The two had made angels in the snow. Reece had gone home shivering and had to stay in bed for two days with a head cold. Beth had made him a paper angel to watch over him until he was well.

One of his grade school teachers told of a field trip to the beach. Instead of getting in the water, Reece and Beth had built a sand castle half their size. Beth had declared herself a princess and Reece her prince. However, Reece had insisted he was a Knight's Templar.

Not all of the memories were of happy times. He felt her hand in his after her mother passed away when she was barely a teen. He felt her head resting on his shoulder. He felt the strands of her hair falling through his fingers as he gave her solace.

As the people who'd known them both their whole lives continued recounting tales, Reece's mind went on a trek of its own. A trek where each memory marker featured Beth. It appeared he'd been there nearly every major moment of her life. So, why had it taken so long for him to admit his feelings to her?

He wanted to ask her. But now wasn't the time. They weren't alone.

Reece's gaze swept the crowd looking for his wife. She'd been at his side most of the night. At some point, they'd become separated. He felt an emptiness beside him that was just her shape and height.

He found her sitting in a group of older women. The women spoke animatedly to her, over her head, and across her. For her part, Beth smiled politely, her eyes blinking slowly as though the lids were heavy.

It had been a long day. He knew that she was tired. He could see the exhaustion written across

Beth's face, but the smile on her lips said she'd fight through it. It wasn't the first time he'd seen that expression.

More flashes of memory skittered through his mind. He saw Beth's face in the firelight. He saw her smile illuminated by a movie screen, a television screen, a computer screen.

With each instance, she looked up at him with the same heavy-lidded smile. Beth, he remembered, was not a night person. She was up with the dawn, eyes bright. But when the sun set, so did she.

"You ready to go?"

Beth turned to him. Her eyes lit when she saw him, the weariness receded to the corners of her gaze until all traces were gone. She nodded enthusiastically. His heart filled with knowing that he could incite that emotion in her, that she clearly wanted to be alone with him as much as he wanted to be alone with her.

Beth said their goodbyes for the two of them. Reece couldn't remember a single name of the people he'd been chatting with the entire day. No one appeared to take offense. They all gave him encouraging smiles and nods.

Reece took Beth's hand as they walked across the dark pastures. The newlyweds were silent, but it was a comfortable silence. A silence of two people who knew each other.

Arriving at their front door, Reece hesitated. Should he carry her over the threshold? He knew the answer was yes. Beth was traditional in that sense.

"Reece? What are you—ah!"

He swept her off her feet and into his arms. Her weight was slight. She felt right in his arms.

"You'll hurt yourself," she protested.

"I only hurt my head."

"You don't have to do this." She continued to wiggle in protest.

"I have to do it right," he chided. "We're only getting married the one time."

Reece carried his bride over the threshold. Once inside, he didn't want to put her down. There was so much he'd lost, but this he knew for certain; he never wanted to let this woman go.

Her arms were wrapped around his neck. Her face tilted back as she gazed up at him. Her lips were there for the taking.

He could take them. She was his wife now. She was also willing by the look in her eyes. So he took.

Their first kiss in front of the entire town had been sweet. This kiss warmed him down through his fingertips and down to his toes. His knees felt weak, and so he put Beth down. But he didn't stop the kiss. He deepened it, drinking from her like a man taking his first sip of cool water.

He felt alive for the first time since he'd woken up. This was what he was born for, kissing Beth Barrett.

No. She was Beth Cartwright. She was his wife. He could kiss her all night. He could even do more.

As though she'd heard his thoughts, Beth caught her breath. She pulled away from him. But only her mouth.

They both were breathing hard, chests panting from their shared desire. Beth rested her hands on Reece's chest. She didn't press against him, but Reece got the signal that she didn't want him to advance any further.

He could've pressed his suit. There was no fight in her, as evidenced by the way she laid her forehead against his chin. Having not had his fill of her, Reece pressed his lips to her forehead. He wrapped his arms around her waist. They stayed like that while he waited for another signal, either for his retreat, or hopefully, for him to advance further.

Though he wished for one outcome, he would

honor either option. And then Beth did something he wasn't expecting. She giggled.

"I never thought this would happen," she said. "I can't believe I'm finally kissing you. I can't believe I'm your wife. It's a dream."

"No," he said vehemently. "Please, no. I was asleep for days. This has been the best part of waking up."

She gazed up at him, open and vulnerable. Her fingertips curled at their place on his chest. Her lips trembled as she spoke to him.

"I love you. So much. I've never said it to your face. I thought I'd never have the chance." She took a deep breath. The next time she spoke, there were no tremors. Her voice was resounding and sure. "Reece, I love you. I've loved you all my life. I'm ready to give myself to you."

Reece opened his mouth to say the same. She'd already said the words. He had the script for what he needed to say.

But nothing came out.

He took a deep breath. A tremor ran through him as he gulped down a breath. When he tried again, his voice caught on something. The only sound that came out was a squeak.

Beth's face fell. It was like watching a rose wilt in

the moonlight. One by one, the petals fell, leaving the bare stamen of the flower exposed.

Her hands recoiled from their place at his heart. She stepped back. But Reece didn't let her get far.

"Beth, I ..."

"Don't." She stiffened her fingers and pressed her palms into his chest. "Don't say anything."

"I have to."

"Reece, please." Her hands balled into tight fists over his heart. "It was too much. I shouldn't have said those things. It's been a long day. We should get some rest."

She stepped toward the spare room. Reece wasn't sure what to do. He knew that sleeping together was out of the question tonight. But he knew he couldn't let her go to bed thinking he didn't care for her.

"Beth, what you said was perfect. You're perfect. You're the first thing I wanted when I woke up. You're the first thing I've thought of each morning since I've been awake, even back in the desert. Tomorrow will be no different for me."

She turned to him, a bright ray of hope in her eyes. Reece closed the distance between them. He pulled her to him, pressing his lips to her forehead again and reinforcing his brand.

"I'm not the same man you fell in love with. I'm

sure you've changed too. But I know with everything in me that you're the woman I'm supposed to be with. Please believe that."

"I do."

He smiled down at her. Then he pressed another kiss to her lips, just a small one. He knew that if he lingered, he would get no rest tonight.

"Sleep well," he said, releasing her. "We'll start our new life together in the morning."

CHAPTER FOURTEEN

She was an idiot.

Reece had been kissing her. It had been better than her wildest dreams. Better than her waking wishes. Better than she could have ever imagined.

And then she'd opened her mouth and ruined it.

Did she really have to make her declaration of love right at that moment? It couldn't have waited until they had been married for, perhaps, a full day? She couldn't have maybe waited until morning to lay it on thick and then make him run for the spare bedroom?

But another part of her revolted. Reece already knew how she felt. She'd written it all down for him. He had the letter to prove it. But saying it all like that, while standing face to face with him, without giving him time and space to compose his own thoughts, it had been too much.

Beth tossed and turned under the coverlet in the unfamiliar bed. The full bed was far too spacious for her body. She felt drowned in the expanse of sheets.

The day had been perfect. Despite all of the gaffs. The dress, the shows, the vows, her father turning up and giving his blessing. But also Reece.

He had been so attentive to her throughout the entire day. He'd kept his hand at her back for most of the day. When they'd been separated, she'd often glanced up to catch him seeking her out. When he'd find her, he'd narrow his gaze, as though asking if she were alright. She would nod. Fifteen minutes later, he'd do it again; seek her out and inquire after her wellbeing.

Now she was alone, in a large bed, tangled in sheets, chiding herself for jumping to a conclusion during his hesitation. Beth ran her hand over her face. The cold touch of metal opened her eyes. She gazed at the ring that Reece had chosen for her. She wasn't sure how he'd gotten it so quickly nor where from. But it was perfect.

The colorful ring was exactly what she'd have chosen for herself. It proved that the Reece she'd known all her life, the one who knew her, was still in there somewhere.

Some part of him wanted her. The problem was she couldn't get that shell-shocked look he'd worn when she'd declared her love for him out of her mind. She'd hinted at her feelings to him once years ago. Just once. It was enough.

He'd given her the same look he'd given her tonight. Back then, she hadn't been as explicit in her ardor. His response had been to call her his sister. That had doused cold water on the flame she'd been trying to stoke.

She'd been able to laugh it off that one time. She couldn't laugh about it now. Not with his ring on her finger and him in the next room.

A choked sound came from the other room. A loud gasp, like someone who'd already let out a string of chuckles and was now trying to catch their breath.

Wait? Was he laughing? She could hear him in the next room. There were more gasps. Followed by a series of short bursts. It could have been coughing, but it sounded more like chortling.

Were the chuckles at her expense? There was something off about the sounds. They didn't sound joyful or chiding. They sounded painful.

Beth rose from the bed. She put her bare feet on the floor and held still to listen. She wanted to be sure. She'd embarrassed herself enough for one night.

The next burst of sounds confirmed it. Those weren't chuckles. They sounded like moans of pain.

Beth rushed out of the room. From the hall to the living room, the house was dark. As she stepped closer to Reece's room, she saw that no light shone from beneath his door.

She lifted her fist and knocked. No response. No acknowledgment.

She was on the verge of convincing herself that she'd heard things. She was about to turn away. But then she heard it again; the unmistakable cry of pain.

Beth tried the door. It was unlocked. She hesitated for only a second, wondering if she should invade his privacy without permission. She'd been hasty in everything she'd done so far, why stop now.

She pulled the door open to a thick darkness. It took her eyes more than a few seconds to adjust. And then she saw him.

Reece lay writhing beneath the sheets. His features were contorted in agony. With his next move, he kicked off the sheets, and Beth got a clear sight of his bare chest.

Her husband was in sweat pants and bare feet. She wasn't sure why his bare skin shocked her. She'd seen him in swim trunks more times than she could count.

He moaned again, the sound sent a shudder through her body. She felt the echo of pain run down her spine. Whatever was there in his dreams was not pleasant. His fists balled, and his legs pumped as though he were trying to get away from whatever was behind his eyelids.

Beth took a step toward him and stopped. Pastor Patel had told her to approach soldiers cautiously when they were unaware of her presence. But she couldn't bear to see Reece in misery.

Reece had never been a violent man. He'd never do anything to hurt her physically. She just needed to make sure he knew it was her.

She knew that awakening to the darkness would disorient him. Reaching out, she felt for the wall paneling. Her fingers hit pay dirt when she found the light switch. She flipped it up, and light flooded the room.

Reece roared awake. He threw his arms over his face. "Off. The lights. Off."

"Okay, okay."

Beth fumbled for the switch. Once the switch was down, the room was cast back into darkness. She heard Reece panting as though he'd been running for his life.

"Reece, are you okay?"

Stupid question. Clearly, he wasn't. He didn't answer. He was too busy gulping air into his lungs.

"Should I call Pastor Patel? Or Ruhi?"

Ruhi would be a better choice. The nurse, who lived on the ranch with her soldier husband and their infant, was just a few doors down.

"Beth?" Reece breathed. His voice sounded broken.

Caution told her to keep her distance. Her heart shut that idea down. It was Reece, and he was in distress.

"Beth?" There was a note of panic in his voice now.

"I'm here." She made her way to the bed in two strides.

Before she could climb on the mattress, his arms snaked out and grabbed her. Reece brought her down onto the bed beside him. His hold was a vise grip.

"Don't go," he murmured into her hair.

Beth lay on her back while he was on his side. Their bodies were flush together. One of his arms pressed against her shoulder blades to mold her body into his. Another hand was in her hair, holding her against him.

"It's okay," said Beth. "I'm here. I won't go."

"The light." His breathing remained harsh. "It brings back the memories. Some of them are blinding. They feel like a physical burn. But when you're near ... it doesn't hurt as much. It's like your light is brighter. It's how I knew it was right to reach for you on that first day. And now."

Reece's heart pounded against her chest. She was certain he felt hers pounding the same rhythm. The organ was trying to get out of her chest and go to him.

"Stay with me?" he begged.

"Forever," she agreed.

Reece wrapped himself around her and was asleep in minutes. For the remainder of the night, they rested peacefully inside each other's arms.

CHAPTER FIFTEEN

"Did I ever tell you how we ended up just outside an insurgency stronghold?" said Sgt. Chase.

All eyebrows were raised in incredulity. Except of course for Ortega and Lucas. Reece lifted one brow. Though he didn't remember the story, he knew the significance of nearly crossing into lands overrun by insurgents.

The five permanent male residents of the Purple Heart Ranch and the four men of Reece's fire team were gathered in one of the barns. That particular barn had been remodeled into a gaming room. There were three flat screen televisions. An array of gaming consoles from Play stations to Nintendos to an old fashion Atari.

Surprisingly, Reece remembered the game he was playing. He'd beaten Specialist Sean Jeffries a number of times. Jeffries could've grumbled that his lack of concentration was due to having a baby at home, but he didn't. He took his licks and got up again.

Reece liked the man. Jeffries was quiet and didn't ask him any questions. None of the men in the room tried to get Reece to talk about his memories. Not even when they recounted times in the military, like now.

"We were patrolling a border city, but something happened to the military charts." Sgt. Chase slid a sideways glance over to Ortega.

The man's dimples made an appearance as he spoke. "I still maintain they were in my bag when we left the base."

"So, this fool," Chase spoke over Ortega, "pulled up Google Maps."

"He didn't," groaned Sgt. Banks. The man rubbed his hands over his eyes.

"As you know," Chase continued, "Google Maps isn't known for its accuracy; hence, you're often rerouted. We just so happened to be a mile and a half off in accuracy."

All the men groaned now.

"We nearly caused an international incident because we used a navigation system that's best for locating the closest Starbucks and not military patrol routes."

"Hey." Ortega lifted his hands, as though in defense of his actions. "A good, dark roast is worth fighting over."

All the men laughed, Reece included. He couldn't remember the incident, though it would have happened during the time he was on the team. Still, Reece enjoyed being amongst the men. It felt right. Mostly. He couldn't shake the feeling that something was missing.

"Married life is agreeing with you," said Ortega as he came over and slumped down in the chair Jeffries had just vacated.

Reece nodded. His marriage to Beth was agreeing with him completely. He'd been enjoying wedded bliss for only two days.

He and Beth had developed a routine. They had breakfast together in the mornings, discussing various topics. None to do with his memories or lack thereof. They had quietly decided to start with the present and forge a new life together with new memories.

During the day, Reece milked cows, rode horses,

and did other chores around the farm. Beth went off with Reegan to the gardens. Although she came back each evening without a spot of dirt on herself, so he wasn't sure exactly what form of gardening his wife was or wasn't doing. Then the two had lunch with the others in the afternoon.

In the evenings, they'd make dinner together in their small kitchen with produce from the gardens and meat from the farm. Afterward, they'd read the Bible together. That was Reece's favorite part of the day; listening to Beth recite passages from his worn devotional.

When it came time for bed, Beth made sure all the lights were extinguished before climbing into his bed. After a few chaste kisses, they settled their heads on their pillows and were asleep instantly. At least he was. Holding Beth in his arms brought him total peace.

They were taking things slow, getting to know each other for who they were in this time and not in the past. Yet, Reece felt he knew everything he needed to know about the woman he'd given his vows to. All that was left was becoming the man she needed him to be.

Reece wasn't sure who that was now that he'd been discharged from the service. He'd been told he'd had plans to reenlist, but with his current condition that wasn't going to be a possibility.

He and Beth had no worries financially at the moment. They lived rent-free on the ranch, and his pension covered any other expenses they might have. But it wasn't enough to give him a sense of purpose. He just wasn't sure where to look.

"Beth?"

"Hmm?" She turned the page of his Bible looking for the passage where they'd left off the previous evening.

"There's Wednesday Night Bible study at the church," he said.

"You remember that?"

Her thumb and forefinger pinched the page she'd been about to turn. Beth was the only person who didn't have hope in her eyes about his amnesia. She had caution when she thought he might remember something.

"No, I don't. I read it on the church's website."

"Oh," she said. "Yes, there is. It starts in about an hour."

"I'd like to go to church," said Reece.

"To ... our church?"

Reece nodded. "I only have happy memories about the church. It's probably because you're in most of those memories. All of my memories of you are always good ones."

"I'm not perfect." Beth shut the Bible with a decisive thunk. "I have my vices. You and I have even had our share of disagreements in the past."

"I know."

That caution showed again in her eyes. Her jaw tightened as though she was holding her breath. She searched his gaze as though she might be able to see what he was remembering. Ever since he'd told her that some memories gave him physical pain, she'd been like one of those gargoyles over churches, watching and waiting to ward off anything that might trespass in his mind.

"I remember the strawberry versus chocolate ice cream debacle," Reece clarified.

Beth blinked. Then an unexpected giggle loosened her clenched jaw. "I can't believe you remember that."

"That was a brutal battle between the two of us. I seem to remember sprinkles being thrown."

"You started it." She grinned, pointing an accusatory finger at him. "We're still not allowed in Mr. Vincetti's ice cream parlor."

"I'm sure when you admit chocolate is best, you'll be welcomed back like a civilized person."

"Never." Her growl was that of a fierce kitten.

Reece loved these moments with her. He preferred nothing better than to remember the good times he'd shared with his wife or to make new memories with her in the safety of their home. But he craved a wider community and deeper relationship with God and church. His church.

As their laughter over the ice cream flavor memory died down, Reece noted the hesitancy return to Beth's features. He wasn't sure why? He thought she and her father had made up at the wedding.

"There's something you should know," she said. "I was engaged."

"To be married?"

She nodded.

"To someone else?"

"The youth pastor." Beth smoothed her hand over Reece's Bible. Peeking from the inside cover was the worn page of the letter she'd written to him. "When you didn't answer my letter, I took it as a rejection. When you went missing, I decided to try and carve out a semblance of a life without you. So, I said yes to Walter."

Walter? What man had a name like Walter? It was a grandpa's name. Reece disliked him instantly.

"When you said you *were* engaged …?"

"I broke it off when you came back," Beth said. "I knew I couldn't have married Walter the moment I saw you again. These feelings I have for you are permanent. They're so big. They can't be ignored."

Reece pulled his wife to him. He set aside the Bible with her love letter to him inside its pages. He took her chin in his hands and brought her lips to his in a kiss.

It wasn't one of their chaste kisses before bed. This kiss was a claiming kiss. Reece pressed his lips to Beth's firmly. He had every intention of leaving a mark. He wanted every man to know that Beth was his.

When he pulled away from her, her breath was ragged, and she appeared a bit disoriented. Reece wasn't. His mind was clear, and his point had been made. Her lips were swollen, and her hazy gaze was focused entirely on him, just where he would always keep it.

"Thank you for telling me," he said. "But what does that have to do with Bible study?"

"Walter preaches at the church. When I decided to marry you, I figured I'd give him some space. That's why I haven't been back."

"You said he was the youth pastor? He's not likely

to be at a nighttime Bible Study. Besides that, you shouldn't run from the place you love because of this."

"I do miss it."

"Me too."

"Then, let's go."

CHAPTER SIXTEEN

Of course, Walter was at the church when they arrived. Because that was just Beth's luck. As Beth and Reece walked down the halls, hand in hand, Walter came out of his office followed by the young couple they'd counseled just a couple of weeks ago. In the fluorescent light of the hallway, a small diamond glinted on Nathalie's left hand.

"They said as long as I get my Associate's degree, and if I can save up enough for first and last month's rent, then we can get married next year."

Nathaniel beamed down at his fiancée. Walter nodded his head. He smiled at the young couple, but the smile didn't reach his eyes. In fact, his features looked a bit worn and haggard.

"We were ignoring faith and hope," said

Nathalie. "We'd planted too many doubts in our parents' minds. Your fiancée was right."

Walter's jaw tensed. His smile dropped by degrees. Then he looked up to find Beth and Reece approaching, and his features went positively frigid.

Nat and Nat looked at Beth and Reece's joined hands. Confusion spread over the teenagers' faces. They looked to each other, then to Pastor Vance. Wordlessly, they made the decision to walk past the new couple and the odd man out.

"Pastor Vance, I'm Reece Cartwright." Reece stuck out his hand. "I'm pleased to make your acquaintance."

Walter looked at the proffered hand. The weariness in his features spread like wildfire. In the end, the man took a deep breath and clasped Reece's hand.

"I thought you lost your memory?" said Walter.

"I lost my memory, but not my way to the Lord. Beth was the guiding light that brought me back home, back to myself."

Walter took another deep breath. A slight sheen of sweat dotted his forehead as though this interlude was exerting him greatly. "God be praised that you are home and well. But I'll need to ask your forgiveness if I can't yet congratulate you on your marriage. I may be a man of the cloth, but I am by no means perfect. I'm suffering from a bout of both envy and jealousy at the moment."

Though Beth stood at Reece's side, their hands still clasped, Walter only looked at Reece. His words were meant for her, but he still hadn't acknowledged her.

"*'And whenever you stand praying, forgive,'*" said Reece. "*'If you have anything against anyone, so that your Father also who is in heaven may forgive you your trespasses.'*"

"Matthew 11:25," said Walter.

Reece nodded.

"You know your scriptures well."

"I was told that I have a B.A. in Biblical Studies. I can remember full passages of the Bible. It's just people and experiences that I'm having trouble with."

"I've only ever heard what a good man you are."

"Beth said the same about you," said Reece. "I hope that one day we might get to know each other better. And I hope that you can forgive her for my trespasses."

Reece inclined his head to Beth. He loosened his grip on her and draped an arm around her shoulder. Beth snuggled into his hold as Walter's gaze found hers for the first time. But only briefly before settling back on Reece.

"I wish the two of you well." Walter turned and went back into his office. He closed the door behind him with a quiet snick.

It was the best they were going to get. The wounds were too fresh. Beth hoped that one day soon Walter would come to forgive her her trespasses. But she knew that day would be far, far into the future.

"That went better than expected," said Reece as he turned her away from the door. "If I lost you to him, I'd be on the floor."

Beth gazed up at her husband. The statement seemed absurd now. No matter how much she would've tried, she would never love another man the way she loved this one.

Reece's blue eyes sparkled as he looked down at her. A warm smile tugged at the corner of his mouth. And then his lips were on hers, brushing lightly.

He hadn't pressed his suit on her these last few days. But neither had he kept his hands and lips to himself. His hands always rested softly, just a hint of weight. However, Beth felt the yearning need of possession in how his fingertips would curl ever so slightly into the fabric of her dress.

His kisses were soft, patient, fluttering touches. Yet the hot breath he'd exhale when they parted always told her the full truth; Reece wanted her as a husband wanted his wife.

Each night he held back. Waiting for … something. Beth wasn't sure what, and she wasn't sure how to ask. With each embrace, with every caress, she knew she wouldn't have to wait much longer.

They entered the Bible study room. It was a relatively full house. Ten people were gathered in the semi-circle of chairs. One of the junior pastors was in charge tonight.

Reece leaned forward as he'd always done in school classrooms. He'd always sat dutifully when he was in church services, following along in the leather-bound Bible that had belonged to his father. But he thrived in these types of lecture settings.

He offered up his thoughts on the night's readings, but in no way manipulated the conversation. He listened to the other parishioners with keen interest. He built on the ideas put forth by the pastor. He searched for deeper context, often pulling in other instances in the scriptures. Soon, everyone was leaning forward and listening to him before offering their own thoughts.

"Did I want to become a pastor?" he asked as they left the study group.

Before Beth could answer, a deep male voice beat her to it.

"No, I would've loved that if you did."

They both turned to the sound of Pastor Barrett's voice. The man was standing at the church's great doors. He was in his shirtsleeves, his jacket slung over his arm and his car keys in his hand.

"You liked the academic side most. The history around the scriptures, the development of the church. Not to mention the cultural aspects of the old world. That's why you began learning the old world languages."

"I speak four languages, don't I?" said Reece.

He repeated the sentence in three distinct languages. Beth couldn't make out any of the harsh sounding words.

"Why don't you two come over for dinner?" said her father.

"You cooked?" asked Beth.

"*Pfft*." Her father let out a harsh breath. "Why do you think I'm inviting you over? So that you can make your old man a good meal."

Beth let go of Reece's hand and snuggled under her father's hold. The three of them walked out of the church and down the street together. It felt like old times. Beth's heart was ready to burst with the joy of it.

While Beth wrangled a meal of baked chicken breasts, roasted potatoes, and green beans, Reece and her father kept up the discussion in the other room. Their conversation lasted all through dinner and beyond. They didn't exclude Beth. In fact, they asked her opinion at many turns.

Beth wasn't interested in the topic. Talking seemed like a chore when she simply wanted to watch, listen, and soak in the scene before her. Her father and her husband at the dinner table, their bellies full from a meal she'd crafted.

A quarter of an hour later, when she saw that the conversation was still going strong, Beth decided to take on another duty that had been hers when she'd still lived at home. She loaded the dishes and wiped down the counters.

Poking her head into her father's office, she saw that it was in disarray since she'd last been home. Even though she was now married, she'd need to make her visits to her former home much more frequent. She knew her father could do without her. He just hadn't adjusted yet, and he didn't truly need to. Beth was happy to manage both households. She certainly had the time, now that she felt comfortable back in both her family church and her family home.

She straightened the books on the shelf, replacing texts he'd used in preparing a sermon last month. She straightened her father's papers, sorting the documents into various piles. There was a separate pile of unopened mail at the corner of the desk. A few bills, a few letters from parishioners, and a few pieces addressed to her. One envelope, in particular, stuck out.

It was army issue.

It was from Reece.

The post stamp was from over a month ago. Sometimes military mail was delayed, especially when it came from overseas. So this would've been from Reece before he lost his memory.

It could be one of his normal letters. They'd written to each other his entire military career, preferring the handwritten notes to emails and phone calls. Somehow, she doubted it was a normal correspondence.

Her fingers trembled as they set to the task at hand. Beth tore the lip of the envelope carefully. The first line tore at her heart.

Dear Beth,

You are my dearest friend. I love you like you were my sister...

She heard the words in her head in Reece's own voice, an echo of the one and only time she'd tried to tell him her feelings face to face. He'd let her down gently then. The letter was a repeat performance.

She didn't read the entire missive. She couldn't. She knew where it would end having been there before.

Beth looked down at the ring on her finger. The one he'd so carefully chosen for her based on the memories he did have of her. He had no recollection of this letter now. But one day, he would.

What was she going to do until that day?

CHAPTER SEVENTEEN

"It really is good to have you back, son."

Reece sat back in the recliner in the Barretts's living room. It felt normal, natural. He was certain he'd done this before. Many times.

The lights were dim. The memories breezing through his mind were easy and non-threatening. He remembered Christmas morning at the Barretts. He remembered Sunday dinners. But mostly, he remembered Beth.

"I admit I had fantasies of you and Beth getting together when you were younger," said Pastor Barrett. "But you always seemed more like siblings than anything romantic."

Reece frowned at the thought. His feelings for Beth were most certainly not brotherly. Though he wasn't about to admit that to her father. Reece hoped that he and Beth would soon take their relationship to the next level.

He'd taken his time with her. Sticking to a few chaste kisses. Tempering his touches and embraces to remain light. He wanted to be sure their relationship was firmly rooted in the present and not relying on the past, especially since he didn't have a full picture of the past. He wanted to be sure that Beth loved him for the man he was today, as he loved her for the woman that she was in this moment.

He felt certain that the mission had been achieved. He believed the next time he took his wife in his arms and kissed her they wouldn't be falling to sleep immediately. Just thinking about it, he felt his cheeks heating, which would not do while he was sitting in front of her father.

Reece turned his gaze to the window, hoping the moonlight scene would cool his ardor. Under the light of the moon, he saw a familiar structure across the street. He realized what the dark outline was.

"Have you been to see it?" Pastor Barrett asked.

Reece shook his head. His fingers gripped the leather cushion of the seat. "I think I should."

"Do you want me to come with you?"

"No," Reece said rising. "Let Beth know I'm outside."

Once outside, Reece barely made it across the street before his knees went weak. He smelled char. Patches of the roof were missing. There was no glass in any of the windows. Two black smears ran down the front of the house. It was as though happiness leaked out of the structure. It looked war-torn.

A light breeze blew on the wind, ruffling the ghosts of memories around his mind. Reece saw his parents sneaking kisses on the patio when they thought he and Reegan weren't looking. Another flash showed him and his sister running through the sprinklers on a warm summer's day. Another glimmer displayed him and his friends playing a game of soldiers where they lined up and marched across the lawn.

Reece walked closer, his feet making a slow march toward his past. The memories were calling to him, like a blow horn. They pushed at the back of his brain, trying to make their way forward.

And then an explosion broke the barrier.

Reece's logical brain knew that the sound was of a car backfiring. But the memories took the opportunity to charge forward. Down to his knees, he went, hard. The assault of his entire past flooding his temple shot pain throughout his entire body until he felt like his fingers and toes were the barrel of a discharging firearm.

He took a deep breath, fighting for air, fighting to maintain consciousness. Dirt touched his lips. Concrete abraded his palms. Blinding light filled his eyes.

And then he felt hands on his back. But when he looked up, it wasn't a face covered by cloth like when he'd woken up the first time. It wasn't the face of his sister that mirrored his own. It wasn't the face of his wife, whom his heart had known instantly.

"Mrs. Harrison?"

"Are you all right, dear boy?"

That's what she called everyone; *dear boy* or *dear girl*. Kids were dear to Mrs. Harrison because she'd never had any of her own.

Reece remembered that. He remembered her. Mrs. Harrison, the wife of grumpy old Mr. Harrison. Her husband had only ever scowled at the neighborhood kids, but his wife always smiled and had cookies in her apron.

"You remember me?" asked Mrs. Harrison.

"I remember everything."

He remembered his parents sending him off for training camp. The mix of worry and pride intermingling on their faces. He remembered his first tour and the apprehension he'd felt on the flight overseas. He remembered his first few months on base, making friends, and bonding with his team.

His team; Chase, Lucas, and Ortega. They were his brothers.

He remembered the look in Lucas's eyes just before the bomb had gone off. That look hadn't been in fear of his own life. It had been about Reece, and the knowledge Brandon wouldn't get to him in time.

But he'd come back for him. And now they were true brothers. Reece had lost consciousness in that explosion, and he'd woken with a whole new lease on life.

Now more than ever, he knew what was important. Family. Not just the family by blood, but the family that he'd chosen and those who had chosen him.

His fire team was his family. The men and women of the Purple Heart Ranch were his family. The people of this town were all his family. But most importantly, Beth was his family.

Beth.

He needed to get to Beth. He needed to tell her that he remembered. But first, he had to escort Mrs. Harrison back across the street.

As he deposited the older woman at her porch, she reached into her pocket and handed him a cookie. He returned the warm embrace she gave him, holding her tight as he'd realized he needed a motherly hug. After she was safely inside, Reece turned back to the Barretts.

It was when he passed the mailbox that a particularly unpleasant memory shoved its way to the forefront. The letter. After he'd received Beth's letter, he'd written a response.

The words he'd pressed to parchment seemed like a foreign language to him now. In response to the confession of her feelings for him, Reece had let her down. His words had been as gentle as he could make them. He didn't want to lose her. He prized her friendship above all others. But he didn't have those feelings for her.

Well, he hadn't. Not then. Now? Now she was all he thought about.

What had he been thinking back then? It had always been Beth. True, he hadn't realized it then. Would he have realized it had he not forgotten who he was?

It didn't matter. He didn't want to be anyone other than Beth's husband. That's where his new life began, and he had no intention of walking backward. Then a terrible thought hit him.

What if Beth had gotten that letter?

He remembered writing it. Had he actually sent it? He couldn't remember that.

He remembered his high school gym locker. He remembered his college roommate's middle name. But he couldn't remember if he'd posted a letter that would change his life if it fell into the wrong hands.

And then she appeared in the doorway. Beth peered out into the night. Backlit by the porch light, she looked like an angel. He would've followed her anywhere.

He came to her, needing to be near her but afraid to touch her. She looked so ethereal he was afraid she'd dissolve if he actually reached out to her.

"Is everything okay?" she asked.

She looked worried and unsure. Her gaze flickered behind him. Out of the corner of his eye, Reece saw what caused her distress; the remains of his house. She was worried that seeing the destruction of his family home had upset him.

She was wrong. It was just bricks and mortar. The only thing that could rip his heart out now was her rejection.

"What's past is past," he said. "You're my home now."

She closed her eyes and breathed a sigh of relief. Reece opened his mouth and inhaled her breath. Unfortunately, there was still the smell of smoke and char in the air.

CHAPTER EIGHTEEN

Since their wedding, the past nights they'd lain together Reece held onto her, tightly. To be sure, Beth had wanted her husband to press his suit and claim his marital rights. But he insisted on taking things slowly; on the two of them getting to know each other as they were now.

Beth had been content to play along. So long as he stole kisses from her after breakfast. So long as he opened his strong arms to her each night. So long as he pressed his nose into her hair when their heads hit the pillow.

She could spend the rest of her life receiving light caresses from her husband. She could wait forever in his attentive embraces. She could hold still and tamp down her desire for more interminably, so long as his lips remained pressed against her hair, her cheek, her lips. It was enough.

Tonight, however, he kept his distance.

Not physically. They lay side-by-side. Reece held Beth's hand in his own, but his fingers were not clamped down on hers. The hold was loose.

His head was turned away. He stared up at the ceiling. His brows were pinched together, making an M-shape. More than anything, Beth wanted to reach over and smooth the M out into a placid line. Instead, she kept her hand in his loose embrace.

A light shone into the bedroom. They forgot to turn off the hall light. But Reece hadn't made a single complaint about it. Beth doubt he'd even noticed it.

Had it worn off? Whatever had made him rush into her arms and away from the light. Whatever had made him decide he wanted her in the darkness?

Beth turned away from the light. She unraveled her fingers from his. He did not protest. He did not reach out to bring her back. He barely stirred from his quiet reverie.

She turned over onto her side. Pressing her palms together and resting her cheek against her hands, Beth stared out the window. She blinked, and it was dawn.

She hadn't slept a wink. She hadn't changed position in the night. Turning to face her husband, the bags under his eyes told her he hadn't moved his position or slept either.

She didn't know what to say to him. She wasn't ready to tell him the truth; that she'd received his letter telling her that he harbored no romantic feelings toward her. She likely wouldn't have to. By his avoidance of her last night, something inside him was already coming to that realization.

And then what?

Would they have the marriage annulled? There were grounds for it. Plenty of grounds.

Her husband wasn't in his right frame of mind when he said his vows. The bride had knowingly misled the groom. The marriage hadn't been consummated.

"Beth?"

Beth looked up to find Reece leaning over her. His handsome face gazed down at her, blue eyes filled with concern. His smile was soft, not containing hunger as it had been every night before he closed his eyes after their chaste kissing. He rested his head on the knuckles of one hand while his other hand boxed her in.

Beth wanted to stay in the cage of his arms. She wanted to reach out and press her hand over his heart and keep it there for the rest of their days. Or for just one more day. A few more hours. She'd settle for a few more seconds.

His hand came to her face. His thumb brushed her cheek, just under her eyelid where she was certain dark circles hung.

"You didn't sleep well?" he asked.

"Neither did you," she countered. "Nightmares?" She hoped it was nightmares and not memories.

Reece shook his head. "Too many thoughts."

Beth filled her lungs slowly, then let out the breath before he could speak. "What kind of thoughts?"

He didn't turn away from her. He peered into her. Past the windows of her eyes. Down into the chambers of her heart. Until his light touched her soul.

"You have always been there when I needed you," he said. "I'm very lucky to have had you in my life."

She was a balloon, stretching its confines with the breath of his words. One more syllable from him and she would burst open.

Beth shut her eyes. She was far too overwhelmed. Relief rushed through her, giving her a little room to wiggle.

Maybe it would be okay; when she told him about the letter. Because she had to tell him. She wouldn't have their relationship based on lies and secrets. Maybe he could still love her as more than a friend when he knew.

Reece's hand snaked around her waist. Beth opened her eyes as his long, lean body came in contact with hers from his chest on down to his bare toes. He pulled her to him … and kissed her on the forehead.

She let out a sigh. Her breath hit his Adam's apple. She had the urge to taste the bobbing bit of skin. Before she could act on the impulse, the doorbell rang.

Reece released her. Sliding out of bed, he pulled on a T-shirt to cover his bare chest. In a T-shirt, pajama bottoms, and bare feet, he went to answer the door.

"It's just Reegan," he called a moment later.

"*Just* Reegan," came his sister's indignant reply.

Despite the turmoil inside Beth, she chuckled at the siblings' banter. "I'll be out in a bit. Just gonna shower."

Beth took her time getting out of the bed. She wasn't ready to begin this day, not knowing how it would end. Walking over to the closet, she grabbed her purse from its hook. She took the letter from its depths. Unfolding the missive, she read the lines again.

Reece had said he was a new man the day of their marriage. Maybe he didn't harbor these feelings anymore? Maybe he had developed new romantic feelings for her. It was possible. But she wouldn't know until she brought it to him.

She knew today had to be the day she told her husband about his letter. But the day lasted until 11:59 pm. No need to rush it.

Stuffing the letter back in her purse, she padded into the bathroom on bare feet. The tiled room was cold. Beth decided to indulge and run the shower a few minutes to heat up the room. Realizing she'd forgotten her clothes, she headed back to the bedroom, closing the bathroom door behind her to keep in all the heat.

"Mrs. Clarkson brought these pictures over this morning," Reegan said from the other room. "Nearly everything was lost in the fire; all the photo albums. The neighbors have been looking through their albums and finding pictures with us in them so that we have some memories."

"Oh," laughed Reece. "Is that Martin Burns? He lived four doors down. He cheated at chess. He's working on Wall Street now, isn't he?"

"You remember Martin?" Reegan asked. "He was a cheater, and he does work in New York now. What else do you remember?"

Beth couldn't see Reece, but she felt his hesitation. The floorboards creaked as he rose. Beth ducked into the bedroom. Peering through the crack of the door's hinge, she saw Reece poke his head around the corner and look at the closed bathroom door. After a second, he turned back to his sister in the other room.

"I remember everything," he said.

Reegan squealed. Reece rushed out of Beth's sightline. She heard him hush his sister.

"I don't want Beth to know," he said.

"Why not?" asked Reegan.

Why not? Beth knew exactly why not, and it made her knees weak. It made her stomach knot. It made her heart shatter into a tiny million pieces.

Reece knew. He knew their marriage was all a sham. If he remembered weasely Martin Burns, then he surely remembered that he didn't love her.

Clearly, Reece was trying to figure out how to let her down and get out of a marriage to a woman he didn't love.

Beth couldn't breathe. She had to get out of here. She pulled a dress over her head, sneakers on her feet, and then she opened the bedroom window.

Outside, the ground was still wet from the rain. A puddle of mud lay right under the window. With only a moment's hesitation, Beth plunged herself feet first into the pile of dirt.

Mud splattered all over her shoes, up her thighs, and on the folds of her sundress. She didn't spare a care. Her future was already in a ditch. The rest of her might as well join in.

CHAPTER NINETEEN

Reece shushed his sister, waving his hand at her in agitation. That feeling was another familiar thing; being annoyed by his twin sister. Oh, he loved and adored Reegan dearly, but her songbird voice often carried. This was not a song Reece wanted everyone to hear.

He held up his hand, his fingers splayed. His ears strained to listen for any sign of movement, feminine gasp, or floorboard creaking. He heard nothing, but he needed to be certain.

Balling his fingers into a fist, he looked meaningfully at his sister. Reegan frowned at him. The twin expression of annoyance she felt for him dripping off her features to be replaced with incomprehension.

She wouldn't know that his fisted hand signal meant *stop* in the military. Stop moving, stop talking. That there was possible danger afoot because something unknown was present.

Reece wasn't sure if Beth had heard his confession. He needed to be sure. Sound wasn't enough. He needed a sight line.

On quiet feet, he tiptoed toward the hall. Peering down the passageway, he saw that the bathroom door was closed. From within, he heard the clear sounds of the shower running and saw the steam wafting up from under the door.

She was in there. Had been in there for a while if steam was escaping. He let out a sigh and lowered his hand.

"What's going on?" asked Reegan once he'd turned back to her. "Are you and Beth fighting?"

"No, we're not fighting," said Reece. As a matter of fact, they hadn't said much to each other since dinner last night. Something was on her mind, something she hadn't cared to share with him.

A terrible thought arrested Reece's heart. He pinpointed the moment when Beth went silent. It was after running into her ex back at the church.

Just as quickly as the thought came to mind,

Reece dismissed it. The few furtive glances the Youth Pastor had given to Beth had been filled with a mixture of pain and longing. Whereas Beth had looked at him with only shame and remorse.

There was no passion in her gaze as she looked up at her former fiancé. Not the way she looked at Reece. Not the way she'd looked at Reece their whole lives.

Beth had loved him her whole life. If her letter to him hadn't confirmed it, thinking back on all of their encounters now did confirm it. The woman of his dreams had been in arms reach his entire life, and he was only now coming to realize it.

So, why had she begun pulling away from him last night?

"You guys never fight," said Reegan. "Not for real. Not when you were kids, not when you were older. I don't think you two have ever had a real disagreement."

That was true. Reece remembered when he'd told Beth he was going to enlist. He'd expected her to jump for joy alongside him. Her feet had remained on the ground, her smile had turned upside down. She'd looked at him as though he'd told her there was no Santa Claus—which even as a teenager, she insisted that the jolly old man lived in everyone's hearts.

Aside from her adolescent view of Saint Nick and Christmas being her favorite holiday, Reece knew that the church was Beth's favorite place in the world. She hadn't strayed far from it or this community in all her life. Whereas he'd left and gone half a world away.

Before his accident, he'd planned to reenlist. He'd been convinced that a military career was his calling. He'd confided as much to Beth. It had been the first time she'd lied to him and pretended that she was happy for him.

Was that why she'd clammed up last night? Was that why she hadn't slept? Was she having second thoughts about her marriage to Reece? Was she waiting for the day he announced that he was returning to the service?

He could return now that his memory was back. He could pass a psych evaluation, as well as a physical one. But the question was, did he want to?

"I love her," Reece said.

"I know," said Reegan in that annoying, know-it-all way of sisters.

"No, you don't get it. I *really* love her. Not like a friend or a sister. I love her like a man loves the woman he wants to spend the rest of his life with. The woman he wants as the mother of his children."

Reegan leaned forward, one brow quirked up. "I know. I'm just glad you finally figured it out. Especially before she married Walter. He's a great guy. He just wasn't right for her. It was only ever you for her."

It could've never been anyone else for him but her. He had to hope he'd have come to that realization eventually. He was just thankful that it hadn't been too late as well. He now had his answer on whether or not he would go back into the Army.

Losing his memory had saved his life. He'd always believed that serving his country was the most honorable thing a man could do. But there was a higher calling than that. Something that hit closer to home; serving his family, his community.

"When did you get your memory back?"

"Last night." Reece spared his sister the details about what had triggered his memories to all click back into place. He knew she was still having a hard time with losing their family home to the fire. But now that he was back, they would rebuild. It would take time, but they could all stay on the ranch until the job was done.

"And you haven't told Beth yet? Why?"

"I ..."

Reegan was right. Why was he hesitating? He didn't need any secrets between him and his wife. He gave his sister a hug and peck on the cheek and then ushered her out his front door. With the house now empty except for him and his wife, Reece made his way back down the hall.

The muted sounds of water against tile could still be heard from the other side of the bathroom door. It was an unusually long shower. Beth wasn't as mindful of the environment as his sister, but neither was she wasteful.

He knocked on the door. After waiting a few seconds, he knocked again. Louder this time.

"Beth?"

Still no response.

Reece began to worry. His hesitation lasted all of two seconds before he pulled open the bathroom door. He averted his gaze, but he didn't need to. The bathroom was empty, save a thick cloud of steam.

Reece didn't bother turning off the water. A prickling sensation began at the bottom of his spine. As he took quick steps toward their bedroom, the prickling turned to sharp shards when he opened the bedroom door and found it also to be empty.

Panic set in when he saw the open window. Had

someone taken her? No, that was preposterous. He would've heard something. Even if it were remotely possible, the ranch was crawling with soldiers and veterans.

Beth's purse sat on the bedsheet. A sheet of paper sticking out of its belly. A light breeze ruffled through the open window caused the edges of the paper to flutter. The crackling sound of the parchment in the breeze drew Reece closer.

He gave the edge a yank. Yet the moment his fingers came in contact with the page, he jerked his fingers away as though the paper seared his fingertips. But the sheet was already loose.

There, floating to the ground, was the missive he'd fired off months ago. It landed on the top of his bare foot like a silent explosion. The edges of the pages curled as though the fire of the ink had singed the corners.

Reece didn't pick it up. He wanted to stomp it out so that it couldn't burn the new life he'd woken up to. But clearly, it already had.

So, he had mailed it. And she had opened it. He wasn't sure what had made her run? The letter or overhearing that he'd gotten his memories back.

It didn't matter. All that mattered was that he found her and told her what was in his heart in the present moment, and what he wanted for their future.

He left the room, shouting her name. But she wasn't in the house. He looked in the front yard to see that her car was gone. She was gone.

CHAPTER TWENTY

Beth drove aimlessly. The mud from her skirt smeared her elbow as she turned the wheel in directionless circles. She brushed at the mess of her dress, but the stains weren't coming off anytime soon.

Her mind was blank as she felt her heart breaking into a thousand pieces. Meanwhile, Reece was whole once more. With all his memories back, Reece would surely be looking for a way out of their sham of a marriage.

She should have stayed and faced the mess she'd made. She shouldn't have gotten herself into this mess in the first place. She shouldn't have reached out to him when she knew his heart was not hers for the taking.

But truth be told, it had been worth it.

What was the saying? It was better to have loved and lost. Those words were true.

If she had it to do all again ... well, she wouldn't give any of it up. The few days she'd gotten to spend as Reece's wife were worth the sharp points now piercing her chest.

The nights she'd spent in his arms, the furtive touches, the hungry kisses that were on a leash. Every second of it was worth the pain she was in now. Those memories would have to sustain her for the rest of her life because she was never walking down an aisle again. That would be the real lie; to let any other man believe that she could devote her heart to him.

But also, the thought of a life without Reece in it looked beyond bleak. Her stomach tightened with nausea. Her shoulders felt sore and began to droop. There was a sharp pain in the back of her throat. And her vision began to blur from unshed tears that were very near to spilling from every corner of her eyes.

Beth pulled off the main road. She could stomach being a hazard to herself, but she wasn't about to hurt anyone else. Pulling into an empty parking lot, she cut the engine, put her head on the steering wheel, and let the tears flow.

She cried every tear in her heart, every tear in her soul until nothing was left. She had no idea what she was going to do? She had no idea where she was going to go?

The ringing of bells pulled her out of her misery. Beth looked up to find that she had subconsciously driven herself to the one place where she always felt whole and sure: church.

Catching a glimpse of herself in the rearview mirror, she couldn't help but cringe. Elsbeth Barrett had always prided herself on her appearance. The woman looking back at her was a shell of the prim and perfect pastor's daughter.

Her hair was a rat's nest. She wore no makeup, and the red rim of tears around her eyelids did her no justice. Her clothes and skin were mud splattered.

Normally, she wouldn't be caught dead in the state she was in. Appearances did mean something to her. But right now, she was so far from the woman she'd always portrayed herself to be.

Beth climbed out of the car, not bothering to smooth out her sullied dress or her untidy hair. She went inside in search of her father. She knew now that her father wouldn't say *I told you so* when she confessed her sins about the foundation of her marriage. Pastor Barrett would do what he always did when one of his flock had gone wayward. He would guide her on the best course of action.

Sure, he'd be disappointed in her actions. But Beth was ready to atone for that. She was ready to do whatever was necessary to make Reece happy, healthy, and whole. Because even though she'd gotten the better end of the bargain, her heart had been in the right place. She'd only wanted to look after Reece and be certain he was cared for.

Beth opened her father's office door, preparing to confess her sins. Inside, she didn't find her father. She found Walter at her father's bookshelves.

Twin, long, deep, uncomfortable sighs escaped both Beth's and Walter's lips. A heaviness settled over Beth's feet making it impossible for her to turn tail and run. The tightness in her chest from before made it difficult to take in a cleansing breath to get out any words. She slumped against the door in weary defeat.

Walter dropped the book he held in his hands, along with his own wary expression. He rounded the desk and came to her immediately. "Are you hurt? Are you injured?"

Walter's hands came to her shoulders, caressing lightly but urgently. There was no spark in his touch. Had there ever been?

"You're an absolute mess," he continued as he looked her over. "What happened?"

Beth looked into his eyes. She saw no desire, no passion. All that was reflected back to her was concern and compassion. Regardless of how she had hurt him, she knew that Walter would come to her aide if she were in need.

Beth unfurled Walter's fingers from her shoulder and took his hands in hers. "I'm so sorry for what I did to you."

Walter blinked, once, twice. He reversed her hold. Taking her hand in his, he led Beth over to her father's seat. Then he leaned against her father's desk peering down at her.

"This is about your husband?" Walter asked.

Beth winced at the word. "He's not my husband. Not really."

Walter was eyeing her with caution in his gaze. He held his tongue, just like he did in his marriage counseling sessions. But without the other party there, Beth had all his attention.

"It was all a lie," she admitted.

"Are you telling me you don't love Reece?"

The words were so ludicrous that she laughed. The sound hurt the dry patch in her throat. "I love him with all my heart and all my soul. But he never loved me. Not in that way."

"He seemed pretty full of love for you the other day."

"That was then. This is now."

"What happened in the space of a day?"

"He got his memories back."

"So, the man he was before is not the same man that he is today?"

The throb in Beth's heart moved to her temple. She closed her eyes against the oncoming headache.

"I've never believed in the old adage of love at first sight," Walter continued. "Lust is a spark. Love is a raging fire. It takes a while to start a fire."

"Sure," Beth agreed, rubbing her temples with her thumbs. "Unless you use gasoline."

Walter chuckled softly. It was a nice sound. She'd always liked his laugh. It set her at ease. She might not have loved Walter, but she'd certainly liked him.

"Either way it begins, there must be the necessary ingredients. A spark of lust. A match to capture the flame. Fuel to keep it going. Something must be there. I saw a spark in you that day you broke it off with me. I just realized too late that the spark wasn't for me."

The headache was receding, the more Walter spoke. Beth opened her eyes and took in the youth pastor with new eyes. There had been something between her and Walter. But there hadn't been enough fuel to get through a lifetime.

"That's why I didn't fight when you broke off our engagement. You were revved up, full of fuel. I knew you would never stop loving him, and there would never be room for me. When I saw the two of you together, I saw the same thing in him."

"You did?" Hope sprung like an oil geyser in Beth's heart.

Walter lifted an eyebrow as he regarded her. Beth was instantly chastised by that brow. She knew this conversation couldn't be easy for him. Still, he offered her the guidance she sought.

"I don't know the man he was. But whoever he is now, he loves you. You two were close when you were young. You're different people now, especially with his trauma. That wedding was hasty though. You should get to know one another. Perhaps marriage counseling."

Beth stood. But once she was back on her feet, indecision made her knees wobbly. She shut down her uncertainty and opened her arms to Walter. "I truly hope that one day we can be friends."

Walter reached out and put his hand on her shoulder. Both of his brows raised as his gaze traveled the length of her, taking in her state of disarray. "Maybe ... but not today."

Beth couldn't help herself. She burst out laughing. So, she didn't hear the door creak. She wasn't sure how long Reece stood there on the threshold gaping at Beth standing close and laughing with her ex-fiancé after running out on her husband.

CHAPTER TWENTY-ONE

*R*elief.

That's all he felt when he saw her standing with Pastor Vance. Reece ignored the hands that were on her shoulder. Beth was his, and he didn't doubt that. The only thing in doubt was what she believed he felt for her since she'd read that letter. By the shame and guilt that clouded her features, Reece could hazard a guess.

"Will you give us a moment?" Reece asked Vance.

The man looked at Beth, as though asking for her permission. Beth gave him a nod. With a squeeze of her shoulders and a nod to Reece, the pastor left the room.

Reece closed the door to the office before making a beeline for his wife. Before he could take her into his arms, she hopped out of his path and went to the window, standing directly in the sunlight.

The glare didn't give him a second's pause. He followed her, a moth to the flame of the woman that he would die for, live for.

"Before you say anything," Beth began, "I just need you to know I'm sorry I misled you."

"Misled me?"

"I know you remember everything, so you must remember the letter. You must remember that you don't love me."

Reece leaned forward, boxing her in. The sun cast her in an ethereal glow that he could not look away from. "Beth, I do love you."

"Not in that way." Tears pricked her eyes, and her voice trembled. "Not in the way a husband loves a wife. You told me before that you loved me like a sister. But I had to tell you what was in my heart, and when you didn't answer my letter ..."

She took a deep, shuddering breath. As she let it out, her loose hair fluttered off her cheek. Reece brushed the tendrils tenderly away, tucking her hair behind her ear in a semblance of tidiness. He waited for her to finish, knowing she needed to confess as much, if not more than he did.

"Then I got your response in the mail. It came after the wedding. It was mailed to the house."

He nodded, waiting for her to go on. Instead of giving him more words, her head hung, her chest slumped in defeat. Reece gathered her to him, giving her his strength.

"Beth, my strawberry sweet girl, please let me explain—"

"No." She whimpered, but she didn't fight his hold. "I don't want you to explain. I don't want you to tell me that you'll always love me like a sister because I will never feel that way about you. I love you in the way God intended a wife to love her husband, and it will never change."

Reece saw that he wasn't going to get a word in edgewise unless he took action. His wife needed to be rescued from her insurgent feelings. So, he let his training kick in.

He cupped Beth's face in both of his hands. He pulled her to him and then he kissed her until she went senseless. Once she was gasping for breath, he could finally tell her what he needed to say.

"I wrote that letter. I remember writing that letter. I remember what my feelings were. They're not that now."

"They're not?"

"Beth, it was always going to be you. I didn't realize it until I forgot everything else. My first memory was of you. When I woke up, all I wanted was you. Now that I have my memories back, none of that has changed. I still want you. Forever."

He felt her heart racing alongside his. The only light he saw was the light of hope in her eyes. He could bathe in that for the rest of his life.

"I need to tell you what's in my heart," he said, echoing the words of her letter in his own voice. "I love you. I've always loved you. My feelings for you deepened while I was asleep. I woke up knowing there will never be anyone else for me but you. You are my best friend. I'd like to offer you my heart. But—"

"But?" Her fingers tightened into the front of his shirt a death grip. "No buts. I don't want a but."

"But," he chastised, pulling her closer, letting her know that there was no escape from his capture, "I think Walter was right. I think we need to take some time and get to know each other. I'm not sure about the marriage counseling, but I definitely think we should maybe date for a while first."

"Date?"

"Yes, I'll take you out to dinner and court you and—"

She nodded as though considering his proposal. Then the prim and proper pastor's daughter snaked her arms around his neck. She pulled his head down to hers and claimed him. That answered that question.

"We can date if you want," she said when she released him from a kiss that claimed his body and his soul. Beth's kiss took over his mind replaced each one of his memories with dreams of a future with her. "But every one of these dates will begin and end with a kiss."

"I give you my solemn vow," he said. And since he planned to take his wife out to lunch, he began their date as she requested, with the first of a lifetime of unforgettable kisses.

There were couples all around him. At every turn. In every corner.

Mark had no problem with love. He could even be romantic when the situation called for it. But in this place, on the Purple Heart Ranch, even a casual glance could turn into a marriage. That was a situation he had no interest in.

At least not any time soon. He'd gone from his family's two-bedroom apartment, where he'd been one of three siblings crammed into the second bedroom until he was eighteen. It was all his parents could afford.

The Army had been his escape. Now, five years later, he was out of the military and wondering what to do with his life. More than half of his money during his time in service had gone to his family. With only one brother still at home, they had a more comfortable living, but they were still wedged firmly in the middle of the lower class.

Living on the Purple Heart Ranch had been the nicest accommodations he'd ever had in his life. But even with his meager savings, the price of living here was too high. He was not ready for a bride. He could barely take care of himself.

Still, he'd miss this place when he'd have to leave in a few weeks. Unless he put a ring on some poor girl's finger, his time was up, as per the zoning regulations that came with the ranch. It would be the second time he was discharged from a place he wanted to be.

Mark hadn't wanted to leave his life in service, but his disability had forced the Army's hand. Now, he had no way of providing for his family, or himself. He had no idea what he was going to do with himself?

Going back to his parents' two bedroom apartment and sharing a bunk bed with his sixteen-year-old brother was out of the question. At least he hoped that wouldn't wind up being his only answer.

"Ortega, wait up."

Mark turned to see his commanding officer, Sgt.

Colin Chase jogging after him. Unlike Mark, Chase's family was well off. His family's wealth aside, Chase had been lucky in the blast that had crippled Mark. The officer could return to service if he chose.

"I was thinking of setting up a recruitment office here," said Chase as he fell in step beside Mark.

That was the other think about Chase. He thought about others and how he could help them. The man many of the soldiers on the base called The Terminator actually had a beating heart.

"That's a great idea," said Mark. "A lot of these kids need the direction and the work."

It's how Mark had found his way into the military. Near the end of this senior year in high school, a recruiter had handed him a flyer during Career Day. Mark had read the pamphlet cover to cover. The next day, he'd walked into the recruitment office and signed up.

"I was hoping you might stay and help?" said Chase.

Mark stopped walking. It took Chase a second to realize he was no longer beside him. Chase turned and faced Mark fully.

Mark's palms opened and closed, as though he were grasping for something. "You want me to work with you recruiting men and women into the Army?"

"Yeah, I think you'd be a perfect fit. It won't pay much, but we'll be doing a service-"

Chase couldn't finish his pitch. He'd been attacked with a hug from Mark. It wasn't often that they showed any type of affection, but Chase had just offered Mark a lifeline.

"I'll take that as a yes then?" said Chase when Mark released him.

"Yeah. I'm ready. What do we need to do?"

"Well, we just need some start-up capital. There's a big society party coming up; a debutante ball. There will be lots of upper-crust society there. Those types are always looking for causes to put their money in. I should know."

Chase rolled his eyes. He didn't talk about his family much. Mark knew there was some tension there.

"Anyway," Chase continued. "We just need to put on our uniforms and schmooze some rich folks. Then we'll be up and running in no time."

Schmooze rich folks? As in talk to them and ask them for money? The poor kid that still lived inside of Mark recoiled. But he wanted to do this work. He wanted to give back in the same way that had saved him.

So it looked like he'd be off to the ball; a debutante's ball.

Are you a fan of historical romances?
Especially the ones where an innocent miss and a
reformed rake are caught in a compromising position
during a ball?
Well, get ready for a modern day take on that story with
Every Step He Takes
the eighth book in the Brides of Purple Heart Ranch!

Shanae Johnson was raised by Saturday Morning cartoons and After School Specials. She still doesn't understand why there isn't a life lesson that ties the issues of the day together just before bedtime. While she's still waiting for the meaning of it all, she writes stories to try and figure it all out. Her books are wholesome and sweet, but her are heroes are hot and heroines are full of sass!

And by the way, the E elongates the A. So it's pronounced Shan-aaaaaaaa. Perfect for a hero to call out across the moors, or up to a balcony, or to blare outside her window on a boombox. If you hear him calling her name, please send him her way!

You can sign up for Shanae's Reader Group at http://bit.ly/ShanaeJohnsonReaders

Also By Shanae Johnson

The Brides of Purple Heart

On His Bended Knee

Hand Over His Heart

Offering His Arm

His Permanent Scar

Having His Back

In Over His Head

Always On His Mind

Every Step He Takes

In His Good Hands

Light Up His Life

Strength to Stand

The Rangers of Purple Heart

The Rancher takes his Convenient Bride

The Rancher takes his Best Friend's Sister

The Rancher takes his Runaway Bride

The Rancher takes his Star Crossed Love

The Rancher takes his Love at First Sight

The Rancher takes his Last Chance at Love

The Rebel Royals series

The King and the Kindergarten Teacher

The Prince and the Pie Maker

The Duke and the DJ

The Marquis and the Magician's Assistant

The Princess and the Principal